TIN LILY

JOANN SWANSON

Printed in the United States of America
First Printing, 2014

ISBN 978-0-9903453-0-5

Cranky Owl Books
www.crankyowlbooks.com

Cranky Owl Books

Joann Swanson, Author

Intense Psychological Thrillers

For Ben.
With you I'm all wrapped up in love.

And for Mom.
I wish you were here to see this. I miss you.

ACKNOWLEDGEMENTS

The first people I would like to thank are you, the readers. I've imagined this day for a very long time and I can honestly say it's one of the biggest thrills of my life to know someone is going to hold this book and read my words. Man oh man, I hope that isn't hubris.

I am incredibly lucky to have a number of people in my life who are equal parts encouraging and candid. My husband, Ben, is my first reader always because I know he will tell me the truth and kick my butt if I don't keep going. Thank you for helping me dig deeper and do better. I love you.

Quinlan Lee of Adams Literary was my agent for a number of years and worked so hard to sell *Tin Lily*. I know it was almost as heartbreaking for her when that sale didn't come through. Thank you for all you did, Quinlan. I so enjoyed working with you.

JB Lynn, a talented author and amazing friend, did nothing but encourage me from the moment I considered indie publishing. Thank you for believing in me and for all your advice.

My friends, family and coworkers have been so excited and encouraging. How lucky am I to have this many brilliant cheerleaders on my side?

And, finally, I'd like to thank my mom. What I wouldn't give to share this day with her, to see her hold this book in her hands. I wish we could have had more time together, but I am so grateful for the time we had.

PART I

Oh heart, if one should say to you
that the soul perishes like the body,
answer that the flower withers,
but the seed remains.
– Kahlil Gibran

The phone by my bed is ringing. I'm ignoring it, fussing with my iPod knock-off, cranking the volume on my favorite song, tapping out a rhythm on my open history book. Chairman Mao never knew such musicality.

Mom's voice drifts through my closed door. "You going to get that?"

I ignore her and mouth the words, sing along in my silent way, thrum the glossy pages harder. The song dips and I hear Mom answer. "Hello?"

After a stretched moment with nothing more said, she drops the phone in its cradle and squeaks off down the hall.

The upstairs in our rented house has ancient wood floors, so it's easy to know where someone's tromping. Right now, Mom's in her bedroom and she's cranking her own music. I imagine her there with a pile of laundry—snapping, folding, snapping, smoothing.

The phone rings again. Through my music it sounds like bees in a hive, buzzing their happy song. I lift one hand to pick it up and pop my earbuds out with the other.

"Do *not* answer that!" Mom hollers, as if she's seen me through the solid door. Super Mom with her crazy X-ray vision.

The phone rings ten more times before I lean over and switch it off. The one in Mom's bedroom picks up where mine stopped. Twenty more rings until he hangs up. That's how it is when you don't have voicemail or an answering machine.

All this separation. The phone that lets us be in different houses. My earbuds that keep out the ringing, the yelling. My bedroom door that filters Mom's voice. We check out, disconnect. It's how we deal.

Back to history. I loop my song in my ears and flip forward to where we are now. I'm halfway through Tiananmen Square, reading about that brave guy who stood up to the tanks because he didn't like what his government was up to when someone starts pounding at the front door. Not knocking politely like the neighbors do when they're returning something. All-out pounding like there's a tsunami outside and someone wants in. A tsunami in the desert *would* make for a decent conversation.

Mom's footsteps are loud in the hallway outside my room. "I'll get it!" she shouts and stomp-squeaks down the stairs. I hear her hit the hollow spot on the switchback and then it's silence again until she unlatches the front door.

My song's at its pinnacle for maybe the tenth time today when the yelling starts—muffled with my earbuds in. I shove them deeper and ignore the clenching in my stomach.

"Lily!"

Cringe.

"Lily, come down here right now. It's time you know the truth about your mother!"

He's yelling up the stairs like I'm on the roof. Like I'm on the moon.

"Leave her alone!" Mom hollers.

"Did you know she's hiding money? Did you know she's sleeping with every guy she meets? Did you know you're poor for no reason? For nothing? Lily?" His voice, my father's voice, is going up and up, not just volume-wise, but pitch-wise too. This one thing alone tells me that pretty soon he'll be out of control. Pretty soon he'll be crying on the sofa, begging us to not be separated, saying our being gone is hurting him, trying to get back the control he doesn't have any more.

My fake iPod cracks loud in my ears and I yank the earbuds out, then tuck them down in the open binding between a picture of Tiananmen Square and a page crammed with margin-to-margin text. I've looped my song too many times, made the cheap knock-off angry.

I take a deep breath, plaster a calming smile on my face, get ready to pretend and pacify. This is my mantra. *Pretend and Pacify.* I take one last look at my history book and long for that awful story about the massacre of protesters in China instead of my drunk father downstairs.

I'm at the top of the stairs, listening for Dad's yelling, but it's silence down there. It's taken me less than a minute to get ready, to get here.

"Dad?" My voice, shaky.

The silence presses in, makes me feel like I've gone deaf, like there are a thousand happenings in the air around me, but I'm stuck in this vacuum.

I make my bare feet step down to the first riser. I

make them do it again and again until I reach the landing—the hollow-sounding switchback—where I'll have to turn a hundred and eighty degrees to get to the next set of steps. My hand is on the banister, just barely brushing the silky wood.

"Dad?" I say again. I crouch down and look through the railing into the living room. A hunkered form, something I've taken for a piece of furniture, stands up. I see him now. The light is bright above his waist. Below, nothing but shadows.

"Is everything okay?" I whisper.

"There's nothing left. I'm sorry," my father mutters to himself. Hank Berkenshire: alcoholic, used-to-be artist, harasses us on the phone now that we're on our own.

His words don't make sense. I keep going. One riser at a time. My mind is foggy, isn't getting what so much quiet means. I'm stuck in this one motion—going down the stairs—and everything else gets pushed out. It's my whole life, going down these stairs.

Finally, I reach the bottom and dip my toe into the living room like I'm testing river water. I'm behind a long couch Mom bought secondhand last year. It faces the fireplace, where there's what you might call a shrine. Mom loves photography and she loves me, and when Dad gave her a fancy camera, she combined the two and now there're at least a bazillion photographs of yours truly, and not just on the mantel either. They're hung around the room, around the house, each frame different because she's all about the sale bins and blue-light specials. She makes it work, though. Our house is cozy, warm. It might smell like dog food because of the factory next door, but rented or not, it's ours.

Now Dad's standing in front of the fireplace. "Lily, everything's gone. You, Rachel, Dad. The company. All gone." I don't understand his words, wonder if maybe he's come to tell us he's sorry, to say we can go back to the way things were before Grandpa Henry. Before Dad decided he liked drinking more than he liked us. Before life got so bad we had to leave.

I glimpse facedown frames all over the mantel, all over the hearth. I wonder how I didn't hear them crash.

I wonder how I didn't hear anything that matters.

Shattered glass crunches when he sways. He's breathing fast, hard and his face is reddening past the usual alcoholic blush. The capillaries on his nose are bright, pulsing. I follow the line of them down to the tip, down to his moving, now silent mouth, down to his flannel shirt that hides his booze belly, down to his jeans with dark stains I don't think about, down to his paint-splattered work boots, down to the hearth, down to the coffee table, down to my mom.

She's facing away from me, a curled up potato bug that's gone dry and pulled in all its legs. I know she's dead. I know because of what's spreading around her head. Like a million little kids stomped on a million little ketchup packets.

Dad's now waving a gun around the living room, pointing it at random photos Mom had taken and framed, at the paintings he let us bring to the dog food house when we left, at the tiny metal sculptures he made for me when I was a kid.

"She hated us, Lily," he says. "She thought we were failures."

Pictures on the walls tell a different story.

I'm five. Gap-toothed and grinning at Mom holding the shabby camera she used before Dad gave her the fancy one. Brown polyester pants. White blouse, bell-shaped sleeves. Daisy buttons.

Strawberry-blond hair.

"She didn't care about either of us. She was so selfish."

I'm fourteen. First day in the dog food house. Khaki shorts. Blue T-shirt, sleeveless. Sitting cross-legged on the rug Mom made me. Boxes all around. Sticking out my tongue. Long red hair now, almost to my waist. Happy.

"She knew I needed her. Knew I couldn't handle him without her. One year into two. Two years into nothing."

I'm eight. All three of us. Pioneer Village at Lagoon. Old West clothing. Sitting on fake barstools. Dad's soft smile. Watching Mom watching me. His hand holding a tin gun. Mom's arm loose around my shoulders. Her smile bright.

He points at the couch with his gun. "She hid money." Points at it like right there between the threadbare cushions is a pot of gold Mom's been hoarding. "You're poor for nothing."

He giggles—a dark sound in this house of silence. "Grandpa Henry died, Lil. About time, huh? Guess what else?" He waits for me to answer. I don't. "He lied. He died and he lied and he left us nothing." He picks up a sliver of glass, stumbles to the other side of the hearth, to a canvas set up on a miniature easel. "What?" he says, looking at the threadbare couch from under droopy eyelids. "What did you say?" He nods, turns back to the canvas, slices my painted cheek wide. "We don't paint." Grandpa Henry's voice comes out of Dad's throat. "We don't paint. We are men. We work hard and we don't paint." He slices the other cheek and jabs the glass shard at the empty couch. "Happy now?" He listens, shakes his head, face pinched with pain and rage.

I look away from my going-crazy father and touch the couch. Rough under my fingertips.

Different. Memories twist here. Scary movies. Prophetic now. A man searching for a dead girl. Hiding our eyes behind spread fingers, protected from the blue veins, the foggy breath. Me and Mom—together, safe.

"Lily, what did I do?" He plucks a silver cat off the mantel, turns it over and over. "Where is your mother?" He looks down at himself, at the red stains on his flannel, at his jeans, at the dry paint on his work boots. He swipes at Mom's blood, then stares at his fingers. "Rachel?"

His voice, far away.

I shuffle to the kitchen.

9-1-1.

I wait for the ringing to stop.

"Put it down, Beans." His voice is soft, almost a whisper. He calls me "Beans" because I ate a pound of jelly beans when I was five and made myself sick. There's no affection in his voice like when I was little, though. Twisted anger instead. Crazy.

"Please come to 2119 Oak Street. My father has killed my mother."

My voice, dull.

My soul, gone.

I hear the shot and jump. A big hole in the wall. An inch from my shadow head. A chunk of plaster. *Whack!*

Another shot. Neat hole in the window over the sink. Cracks spread from the empty place, make the window dance and moan. Once sand, uncountable. Now glass, shattered grains. Fragments barely stick. Weakening.

"Why, Beans? Why'd you do that?"

Two more missed shots. One for the pantry, one for the oven.

He comes close, wraps his arms around me, pulls me to him. His smells fill my nose—mint to try to hide the whiskey, paint to cover his pain.

One arm holds me against him. His other hand reaches for a dishtowel and presses it to my back. A pillow for his gun, still damp from Mom doing dishes. "Be over in just a minute, sweetheart." I turn my cheek, rest it on his shoulder, watch the window's empty place. I see a mosaic of fear, of rage, of nothing left.

"I love you, Beans. We'll all be together now. Hold real still, honey." His breath, warm on my ear, the gun's barrel pressed to my back. "See you soon." He pulls the trigger.

Click.

I push away. His face changes.

Rage to hurt.

Blink.

Hurt to rage.

Rage stays. Lifts the gun. Giant black hole. Small gun. Small man. Small bullet. Hand tremors. Once. Twice. Pulls the trigger. *Click. Click.*

He points at the floor. Shakes the gun. Pulls the trigger. *Click.*

He raises the gun. Giant black hole. Pulls the trigger. *Click.*

"Empty. Piece of crap."

Sirens.

He hears them too and circles toward me. He raises his hand holding the gun like a club, like a hammer.

I step away, dodging the gun by inches.

He swings, aims for my head.

I duck and circle to the other side.

"Stay still, Beans." His eyes—squinty, unfocused, bloodshot. He staggers, bumps his leg, almost falls.

I circle to the other side.

"Stop moving!" he screams.

Sirens closer. He glances out the window, gauges. Time running out. He nods at empty air, mutters something, opens a drawer, finds a knife, wobbles toward me. "Damn it, Beans, you don't get to decide. Not you. Not your mother. You stay right there."

I don't stay right there.

He stops, takes a breath. He knows he can't get me, so he weaves to the backdoor. Before he opens it, he turns, raises his hand not holding the empty gun. One finger presses down on empty air. He's taking an imaginary picture. Like Mom with her camera. It means *see you later,* like when I was kid. His eyes are different now, though. The meaning is different, too. The Dad I knew is gone, disappeared into someone else.

The small man goes.

Loud sirens shriek outside. Rotating lights swing in through the windows, showing Mom's blood on the curtains, on Dad's painting of me with the torn cheeks. Shadows change my painted eyes to something else—to something empty. Dad's painting, showing everything he's done.

There are loud knocks at the door.

The door shakes in its frame. The frame is steady.

My focus: only the frame.

I twist the knob.

A fireman dances on rubber tiptoes, swivels around me, runs into the house.

There are two paramedics: one for me, one for the dead. Mine crouches and shines a light in my eyes. "Can you count to 10?" he asks, and "Can you tell me your name?"

You should have asked my name first. Now there's only 1-2-3-4-5-6-7-8-9-10-1-2-3-.

His fingers are warm on my wrist. "Can you hear me?" he says, and "Do you hurt anywhere?"

I hurt. Every inch and every molecule. I am pain.

"No," I say.

"Good, that's good, Lily."

He knows my name. "How?"

"You just told me," he says. "You're a little out of it, kiddo. Don't worry. We'll take good care of you."

There's static on his walkie-talkie.

"Do you need to go?" I say. "It's okay."

He shakes his head and smiles. "I'm right where I'm supposed to be, young lady."

"Okay. But if you have to go, I understand." My voice, far away. His face, swimmy.

"Lily? Lily? Are you with me?"

I touch his nametag. "Jim?"

"Yes, it's Jim."

We're in a moving ambulance. "Where are we going?"

Jim sits back. I can't see him anymore. "To the hospital. We'll get you checked out and make sure you're okay."

I hear static again. Jim talks into something. "Shock, BP dropping –"

"Jim?"

He leans over me again. "Yes, Lily?"

"Where's my mom?"

His face tightens, lips mash together and go white. "Do you remember what happened tonight, sweetheart?"

"Yes, I remember. Is she with the coroner?"

Jim nods slowly. "Yes. She's with the coroner."

"Okay."

He tries to smile. "I'm going to take your temperature now, okay?" He holds up a white plastic something. I nod. He pokes a thermometer in my ear, beeps my temperature, reminds me of better times, of Mom, of Hank when he was still Dad.

I'm eleven. Mom's pressing the inside of her wrist to my forehead—Mom-style thermometer. "You don't have a fever, Lil. Does your stomach hurt?"

I groan like my life depends on it. "Yes. I'll be okay by myself, though. You should go to work."

She sits next to me, most of one hip off because my bed's small. She leans over, puts both hands on either side of my head, lowers her nose to mine. Eskimo kiss. "Tell me what's really going on, Lilybeans. Why don't you want to go to school?"

My eyes stretch big, irises so dark they blend seamlessly with my pupils. They're all black unless you look real close. I have my father's eyes, but they're bigger than his. Soulful, Mom calls them.

"I see you've got your deep pools going there, my girl. Now tell me what's wrong."

"There's a field-trip to the zoo today."

Mom nods, understands right away. "You don't want to stay in the library with the other kids not going?"

I shake my head. "Please don't make me."

She smiles big. "We'll both stay home."

"But work—"

"That's what sick days are for, sweet pea."

She leaves to tell my father we're playing hooky and I snuggle under my covers, thinking how lucky I am to have a mom who understands I can't go to a place where they've put wild animals in small cages. She understands I can't see the defeat in their eyes and not cry for weeks after. She gets it.

There's soft talking down the hall and then Dad's here. "Don't wanna go to school today, huh, kiddo?"

I shake my head and pull the covers to my chin.

"Well, I guess that's all right then. You and Mom have a good day, yeah?"

Dad doesn't make a fuss because he's still sorry about all the beers he drank the night before. He's always sorry in the morning. I reach up, touch his name embroidered on his blue uniform shirt: Hank. "Thanks, Dad."

He gives my hair a ruffle, kisses Mom and leaves.

We spend the day making chocolate chip cookies and watching my favorite movie. We snuggle on the couch and talk about everything except the zoo. It is one of the best days of my life.

The night is quiet in this hospital. Someone (cop? social worker? nurse?) sits next to my bed, only looking up from her magazine when I shift. I don't sleep. I focus on the ceiling tiles and count the holes. My focus: counting. So far 1,039.

I'm at 10,952 and the darkness outside my window is gone when a cop walks in and magazine lady walks out.

His nametag says Newbold, but he wants to be called Officer Archie.

"Do you remember me, kiddo?"

There's nothing in me that wants to answer, so I don't.

"I was there last night. I understand if you don't remember."

He sits in a chair next to this hospital bed. Not

my bed. My bed doesn't have a switch to make it raise up, or a blue blanket with a million little waffle patterns, or a worn-out button with the picture of a nurse.

Officer Archie wants to know what happened, but I don't have the words to say.

He smiles and pats my arm. "How about I say what we suspect happened and you let me know if we've got it right?"

Nod.

Officer Archie opens a little notebook, flips a few pages over and gets down to business. "Now, as far as we can tell, Henry Berkenshire, 38, came to 2119 Oak Street—the house where you reside with your mother, Rachel Berkenshire, also 38—at approximately 6:45 PM last night." He looks up at me. "Is this correct, Lily?"

I stare at him awhile. I keep quiet.

He looks back down. "It appears your mother let your father in." He glances at me again, but doesn't ask me to say if he's right. His voice doesn't accuse, doesn't say it was Mom's fault. Just the facts, ma'am. "Your father then entered the residence, fired off four shots in the kitchen area, presumably chasing Mrs. Berkenshire, finally ending his pursuit in the living room, where he shot—"

I flinch.

Officer Archie doesn't finish his sentence, doesn't need to. He closes his notebook and sits back with his arms crossed. His mouth is hard. His eyes are soft.

They don't know Hank's kitchen bullets were for me.

"Is this what happened, Lily?"

I decide it is and nod.

"Okay, thank you, young lady." Officer Archie takes a deep breath and leans forward. In his eyes I see he's done this a lot, this recounting of the worst kind of awful. There's weariness and sadness and awkwardness. "I understand your parents were separated."

Nod.

"And your father is an alcoholic?"

I watch Officer Archie closely, wonder how he knows.

"We've been in touch with your mother's friends. At her place of work."

I don't say anything.

"The friends are incorrect? About your father's alcoholism?"

Shake.

"Was he drunk last night?"

Nod.

Officer Archie thinks on this awhile, then leans back and says, "Do you have any other family in Utah?"

Shake.

"Any other family at all?"

Nod.

"Someone who would come if we called?"

Nod.

"I'll need his or her name, kiddo." Officer Archie flips his notebook to another fresh page, clips his pen to it, hands it over.

I write down "Margie Hadden," but I don't know her phone number. I write down "Seattle," but I don't know her address. I write down "aunt," but I barely know her at all.

"We'll find her," Officer Archie says. "It might take a little time if she's unlisted."

Nod.

"We have a foster home lined up in the meantime. A social worker'll be by a little later, let you meet Mack and Darcy. Sound good?"

I don't feel anything inside, so I don't nod or

shake or speak.
    I count.
    10,953.

"Lily, this is Mack and Darcy Langhorn." Officer Archie stretches an arm toward two people standing behind him. With the flat light of his eyes, with the straight set of his mouth, with the deep crease of his brow, Mack reminds me of Hank after his light went out. After he went to work for Grandpa Henry. After he decided drinking was better than painting and sculpting. Darcy doesn't remind me of anyone.

"Hello, Lily," Darcy Langhorn says. "It's sure nice to meet ya and we're sure sorry 'bout what happened to your mama."

Nod.

"Don't she talk?"

A hospital social worker—magazine-reading lady—stands at my side and touches her cold fingertips to my arm. "She's still in shock."

"She gonna snap out of it?" Mack-Hank asks.

"It's been a day," Officer Archie says. His voice holds a warning.

But Officer Archie's wrong. It's been twenty-three hours and nineteen minutes. Forty-one minutes shy of a day. I don't say this.

"Lily, Mack and Darcy are foster parents who own a sheep and cattle ranch down by Kanab. They're ready to take you in until we can find your aunt."

You don't keep sheep and cattle for pets. You keep sheep and cattle for killing. Mack-Hank and Darcy's place, it's a million times worse than the zoo.

When I look at the Langhorns and the way their eyes watch me without understanding, I think there's more in me than silence. "Please find my aunt."

The social worker flinches and Officer Archie nods.

"Why's she sound like that?" Mack-Hank asks.

"Shock," Officer Archie says.

I'm to go with Mack and Darcy—temporarily, Officer Archie says. Just until he can find Aunt Margie. I want to stay in the dog food house where we were happy for a little while, where Mom's pictures are still on the walls, where Tiananmen Square still needs reading. But I can't stay. I have no choice.

It's my last few minutes at the hospital and I'm counting the words in a magazine article when Aunt Margie walks into my room. She's wearing a pink T-shirt that says "Metallurgists Rock!" I think this is maybe meant to be funny—a pun or something. Margie's small, smaller than me, pretty too, even with red-rimmed, bloodshot eyes. Her dark hair is short now—pixie cut. She looks nothing like Hank even though she's his sister. Margie Hadden. She has a different last name because she got married and then divorced and then didn't change it back.

"Lilybeans?" She gets to me, wraps her arms around me, pulls me against her. Her skin is warm from the early summer sun. "Oh god," she says. "Oh god, how could this happen?"

I'm dead weight, but she holds me anyway. Margie's stronger than she looks. I can't breathe too well, but it's okay. I don't mind Margie squeezing me so hard I can't talk. Her being here means I don't have to go with Mack-Hank and Darcy after all. I stare over her shoulder and see Officer Archie standing in the doorway. He smiles, nods once, leaves. He's proud he found my aunt.

"Are you okay, Lil?" she asks when she pulls back. Her eyes don't leave mine. She's trying to see where I've gone.

"I'm okay," I say.

She brushes hair out of my face. Her fingers are rough and soft. "My brother did this? Hank, he did this?"

I don't answer. Her eyes are cornflower blue like Mom's, but flecked with gold too. The cornflower sends a sharp ache where my heart used to be. My focus: the gold.

"I'm so sorry," she says. "Oh god." Her voice hitches. I see the panic coming on and look at my lap, at the open magazine on my legs. I listen to the *whir, whir, whir* of the air conditioner, the buzzing florescent light overhead, the scrape and clang of the hallway.

"What happens now?" I ask when she's quiet again.

Margie stares at me and her eyes are huge. The gold reflects, refracts, tells me what's inside my aunt—fear.

"I don't know exactly. The police officer outside told me it'll take them awhile to finish up their investigation."

To find Hank, she means, but doesn't say.

"Okay. Can you stay?"

"Of course. And when everything's finished, you'll come to Seattle with me."

"Are you sure?" Margie's never had a kid. I'm not a handful or anything, but it's big going from no kids to one.

"I promised your mother," she says softly.

I know my face is a question. I know Margie sees that.

"Your mom asked me to take care of you if anything happened to her. It's how I knew something had, sweetheart. Your mom and I check in every week and I couldn't get a hold of her last night."

I decide not to think about Mom's cell phone playing her favorite song in its tinny way, only her recorded voice left to answer who's calling. I focus on Margie's words. *Your mom asked me to take care of you if…* "Did she know Hank would do this?"

"No, of course not," Margie says. "No." She shakes her head hard. She's trying to convince us both. "She was talking about accidents, not this."

"Okay." Margie and me, we watch each other, and finally, I ask the question that's pushing to get out. "Could we stay here? Me and you?"

"I'm sorry, sweetheart, but no." She looks around the hospital room, out the window, back to me. Her face is pinched. "I can't move back here and I think it's better if we go."

I look out the window and don't say anything.

"Your dad and I haven't spoken since we were kids." Her voice turns to a whisper. "I tried, but he refused. Tried for years. He couldn't forgive me." I don't know what Margie means by this, but there's no curiosity in me to ask. "Anyway, he doesn't know where I live, if you're worried about that."

She waits for me to say something. I keep quiet. "Officer Newbold doesn't think you're in any danger." She tugs on my chin so I have to look at her. "He believes this because Hank left you alive. Lily, if your dad tried to hurt you, it's important you say so."

"Because they'll give us protection?"

Margie shakes her head. "No. I guess Hank left so much evidence behind it's doubtful he'll have a decent defense if the case goes to trial. Officer Newbold said they don't put people in witness protection who won't be needed as a witness."

"Then why?"

"Because there are other ways to protect you. The Langhorn couple—"

"They kill sheep and cows there."

Margie nods slowly. "I know, but their farm is remote and Hank would have no idea how to find you."

"He didn't try to hurt me, Aunt Margie. I promise. Please don't make me go with the Langhorns."

Margie wraps her arms around me again. "No, Lilybeans. I won't. I promise."

There are no words left in me to say how much I can't go with Mack-Hank and Darcy. I think Margie, with her shaking and crying, understands. Not like Mom understood about the zoo, but close.

I'm not afraid of Hank coming for me. I'm not anything. Emptied out. Gone. My own version of a dried-up potato bug.

There's lint on Margie's shoulder—blue, a little white mixed in.

My focus: Margie's blue and white lint.

They let Margie take me after a social worker says it's okay. We go straight to a downtown hotel where she wants to stay. We share a room because Margie doesn't want me out of her sight. She slides a plastic card into the key slot, opens the door and waits until I'm inside with my blue hospital bag full of too-small clothes from Officer Archie gathering them up at the dog food house. Too-small clothes that won't do me any good in Seattle. I need Mom's things—the sweater she knitted me, the rug, her pictures. Mostly I need Margie to answer a question.

"Why?"

Margie stops digging in her purse where she's standing at a little desk crammed in a corner of the room. She turns slowly toward me. I see by her face this one word is enough. She understands.

"Did you know Grandpa Henry died Sunday morning?"

Sunday. The day Hank came with his gun.

"Hank said Grandpa Henry was dead."

"When?"

I tell her with my eyes not to make me say.

"I see. Did he say anything about Grandpa's will?"

"Only that there was nothing left."

Margie paces the room, holding a tiny metal box in her hands and muttering to herself. She turns the box over and over like Hank did with the cat at the dog food house. I think she's working out what to say or what not to say when she stops in front of me with her hands cupped around the box. I see flashes of silver between her fingers. "Your dad expected an inheritance from Grandpa Henry."

"I know."

I know because Hank went to work for Grandpa Henry's company even though Mom said don't, even though Grandpa Henry disowned Hank a long time ago because he wanted to paint and not install rain gutters. Even though Grandpa Henry was poison.

"Pure poison, Hank. Don't do it. We'll survive. We don't need his money."

Dad's face is buried in his open hands, his shoulders slumped. "You think I want to, Rachel? He's sick. He needs me." Dad drops his hands and looks up at Mom. With his own deep pools, he begs her to understand. "One year. I bet he won't even last that long. One year."

"You can't predict that, Hank. The meanest cling to life and there's no one meaner than your father. Don't do this. He'll poison you. He'll poison us."

Dad shakes his head. "I won't let him near you two. He'll never come here."

Mom turns away and now her shoulders are slumped. "He won't need to. Have you forgotten how he treated you? And Margie? Your mother? He leaves no one untouched. Don't do this."

Dad gets up from his recliner and crosses to Mom. "I won't let him affect us. I promise. You know how much we need this. If I get back in his good graces, he'll reverse the disownment and leave me the company. It's worth a year, don't you think?"

Mom leans into Dad, resting the back of her head against his shoulder. "No, it's not worth it, but I think you've already made up your mind. One year. But if..." She turns and looks over Dad's shoulder at me. I pretend to read, to not listen. "One year," she says.

But it only took Grandpa Henry six months to wreck Hank and six months after that for Mom to say we were leaving and another year after that before Grandpa Henry finally died. One year into two, two years into nothing.

Margie's mouth is moving. I hear bits and pieces as I try to catch up. "...inheritance from my parent's estate... huge trust... left us out completely."

I think about the unfussy house I visited with Hank once without Mom knowing—the front porch creaky, all sagging wood and U-shaped steps from so many years of tromping up and down, paint peeling in strips off the siding, the kitchen so old you could smell what was for dinner ten years before. I remember Grandpa Henry sick in bed, a nurse sitting at the kitchen table, her bags packed. Dad was always having to find new nurses for Grandpa Henry. He didn't treat people too well. Never even talked to me while I was there. Not once.

"Grandpa Henry had an estate?"

Margie laughs. Not a good laugh—a twisted, angry laugh. "The old man had a lot of money and the company was worth a fortune."

"He didn't leave it to you and Hank?"

She shakes her head. "Not a cent. I think it may be why your dad did what he did, as much as you can name a reason. I had a call from Grandpa Henry's lawyer before I left Seattle. Hank insisted on a reading of the will hours after Grandpa Henry died. I think he thought—"

"Wait." I hold up my hand to stop her talking.

I take a minute to let her words sink in—the words about Hank coming because Grandpa Henry left him nothing, the words that tell me why. I hear a buzzing and bat at my ear. There's nothing to bat. It feels like a bee's climbed right inside my head and is knocking around in there like it's confused or drunk. "Hank came with his gun because Grandpa Henry didn't leave him any money?"

"I think so," Margie says, but her voice is far away now.

"What did Grandpa Henry do with his money?"

Margie shakes her head. "That's enough for now, kiddo. You're pale as a ghost." She puts one hand to my cheek. Does she feel me buzzing? All these bees under my skin, thrumming inside my head, filling me up with nothing.

I disappear for a little while. I go where it's quiet.

"Lily?"

I blink hard and look around the hotel room, then back to Margie. "Yes?"

"Where'd you go?"

"Nowhere."

There's fear in Margie's eyes. "I've been calling you. You checked out."

I look at the clock sitting on the crammed-in-the-corner desk. I don't know what time it was before, so it doesn't help. "How long?"

"Oh, not long—a minute or two."

"Did I fall asleep?"

Margie shakes her head and squeezes my hand. "No, kiddo. Your eyes were open."

"Okay."

"Do you remember anything?"

"Just talking about Grandpa Henry's money is

all. And the bees."

"Bees?"

"Like in a hive. I thought we had one in here."

"You heard or saw them?"

"Heard. The buzzing was soft for a little while and then it got loud and then it was quiet."

"All right. Do you hear them now?"

"No."

We look at each other. Margie's eyes tell me she's scared of what happened. I don't remember. I can't help her not be afraid.

We're sitting, not eating dinner at the hotel restaurant—grilled cheese for me, salmon for Margie. My bread is white, the cheese is yellow. The yellow reminds me of the daisies Mom used to bring home sometimes. Daisies sitting in a vase like there was no awful coming. Just sitting, sucking up water, waiting until the little life left in their stems and petals petered out. Daisies and melted cheese, both dead and waiting. My focus: the bread.

I think it's been three days, maybe three weeks. I'm not sure.

"I need my books, Mom's sweater, my rug," I say.

Margie pulls out her cell phone, presses a few buttons and talks for a minute.

"Officer Archie says it's okay. He'll meet us

there."

"Okay."

I reach inside my pocket. Empty. It's where I keep my house key. I try to remember these aren't my normal clothes. I try to remember this isn't my normal life.

I check my pocket again.

We drive to the west side of Salt Lake City. The dog food factory is going, spewing white steam and thick stink into the sky. I sniff my new T-shirt. No dog food smell. It'll be there by the time we leave.

Margie drives a rental car up to the curb out front. Mom's car is in the driveway. I'm sitting with my hand half-raised toward the door handle and trying to remember she won't be taking her car to work anymore or the bus when the old heap breaks down. She won't be walking during good weather or having coffee breaks with her friends at the newspaper. She won't be anything anymore.

"You sure you want to do this, Lil?" Margie says. "Because I could just run in and grab up anything you need."

The house looks sad, like with Mom gone it doesn't know how to be a house anymore. The drapes are drawn and yellow crime scene tape crisscrosses the red door. Mom likes everything open.

"So we can play with the sunshine, Lilybeans, and have the outdoors right inside with us."

Hank's rage keeps everything closed, locked up tight. A rage mausoleum.

I pull on the door handle, send out a little hope that I keep it together, forget to answer Margie.

We walk up the front sidewalk—chipped

concrete with old drawings, painted pictographs to tell us about the kids who lived here before. Mom never wanted to scrub them off.

"Those kids put their whole hearts into their sidewalk art. We'll enjoy it and imagine what they were like. What do you think? I'm guessing that pony with the pink mane was painted by a little girl who loves horses."

"That's a pretty good guess, Mom."

"Smart Alec."

"Seriously. Your mental skills are staggering. I never would've guessed that."

"You know what this means."

"Don't you dare."

"You asked for it, kid. Tickle time."

Officer Archie stands on the porch guarding the empty house. His hair is dull brown, like he hasn't washed it in a week. Even the sun can't make it shine. I don't remember his dull hair. I remember his soft eyes, his Mack-Hank warning tone, his understanding.

"Hello again, ladies," he says. He reaches for one corner of the crisscrossed tape. "Please take what you want from your room, Lily, but don't touch anything else. Understand?"

"Okay."

I walk across the threshold first. Margie and Officer Archie come behind. To my right I see the empty place where plaster was. I see the window—a mosaic of splintered glass, grains of used-to-be sand still clinging to the sill and frame, still hoping for wholeness.

To my left is the transformed living room. There's plastic everywhere. Plastic covering Mom's red halo, covering the pot of gold between the couch cushions.

The walls are bare, the shrine gone, pictures and paintings and little metal sculptures all vanished into the ether. "Where is everything?"

Officer Archie disappears behind the breakfast bar, then comes out with a big box in his arms. "We thought you might like to take them. I hope it's okay we packed them for you."

"It's okay," Margie says. "Thank you for gathering these up." She plucks something out of the box, studies it closely and looks up at me, her eyes surprised. "Did your dad make this?" She holds out the tiny silver cat.

"Hank," I say. "Yes."

She wraps her hand around it tight, tight, tight until her knuckles turn white. Then she relaxes her fist and puts the cat back in the box Officer Archie's still holding.

I know Hank's cat has made my aunt mad, but I don't have the curiosity in me to ask why. I slip my feet out of the flip flops Margie bought me and walk barefoot toward the stairs.

"There's broken glass—"

"Not here." Broken glass over there by the mantel. Facedown frames removed, put in a box, gathered up like they don't hold fifteen years of everything that was my life.

One step, another. Two steps, another.

I stop behind the couch and touch its rough fabric.

"Look at this couch, Lily! It's not too bad. Maybe we can reupholster it someday. I'll take a picture, see if the color works in our new living room." Click. Snap.

Margie's breathing gets noisy. She's seen Mom's red halo through cloudy plastic, an arc of dried blood that says she used to be here, but now she isn't.

My focus: the couch because Mom's dead blood starts the bees up again.

But pretty soon there's paint and mint and whiskey. Pretty soon I see Hank sitting on the hearth, his back to the fireplace, his hand waving a tin gun. Then a paintbrush. Gun. Paintbrush.

Gun. *"One year into two, two years into nothing."*

Paintbrush. *"Hold still, kid. Noses are the hardest to get down."*

Gun. *"Lily, what did I do? Where's your mother?"*

Paintbrush. *"Lift your chin just a touch, Lilybeans. And for god's sake, smile. Sitting for a portrait isn't any worse than eating your mom's burnt pot roast, ya Gloomy Gus."*

I'm eight. My prize for sitting for Dad's painting is a visit to Lagoon, where we'll ride the roller coaster and the Log Flume, the Sky Ride and the Tidal Wave. We'll eat churros and ice cream. And later we'll pose for a picture. Mom'll be a saloon girl in a frilly dress and Dad'll be the sheriff, holding a tin gun, wearing a tin badge. I'll be their daughter. When I'm eight I don't want to be anyone else.

I smile at Dad painting my face on his blank canvas.

He smiles back. "Not so bad, huh?"

"Not so bad," I agree.

I watch the way Dad brushes and dabs and sometimes smudges. "Where did you learn to paint?" I've asked before and he always waves my question away, like it's not important. Today he feels like talking.

His eyes go far away, a little squinty—his seeing-into-the-past look. "I used to doodle in notebooks, sometimes in the margins of novels. My mother saw something in those drawings and bought me my first sketchpad when I was six. For years after that, she would sneak me charcoal, pencils, markers, you name it. Eventually, we figured out I was best at this." He points with his brush at the painting I can't see. "While my father was at work, I would paint."

"Grandpa Henry didn't like you painting?" At eight I only know a little about Grandpa Henry—that he's not welcome in our house, that he's mean.

Dad gives me a funny look, like he's searching for the answer in my eyes. "Grandpa Henry believed there was a right way and a wrong way."

"To what?"

Dad rubs the hand holding his brush across his forehead, leaving a streak of red there. "To everything," he says softly.

Dad rubbing his head tells me to stop asking questions. Pretty soon he'll start swallowing a lot and wiping his mouth. He'll say he's thirsty, but not for water. After a few beers, he'll sit in his recliner and maybe nod off, maybe tell me I need to be stronger than I am. Stronger and smarter and not so gloomy. He won't be kidding like when he said Gloomy Gus. He'll be serious and his eyes will glint like two black stones and he'll look different.

I don't ask anymore questions and hope I stopped before the big thirst comes on.

Hank disappears when Margie tugs on my hand. "Lilybeans?"

"All set." I turn my back on the not-shrine and the not-Hank. I step up and toward the hollow-sounding switchback—one-hundred eighty degrees from one set of steps to the next. About face. Hollow thump underfoot. Like a drum. Like a heartbeat.

I'm in the hall that connects our rooms. I glance toward hers. Folded clothes are heaped on her bed, the laundry basket almost empty. A few towels left. Unfinished laundry, frozen in a gone-forever moment. I go there first.

There's just one thing. Only one. I touch the stuff on the bed and run my fingers along the soft bedspread she found on sale last year, then go to the picture on her nightstand. It's one of me and her at the park. A rare one because she didn't like giving up her camera. Another gone-forever moment. I take me and Mom at the park, wrap us up in one of the frayed towels and hold us against my chest. A shield to keep it all inside.

"Okay," I say.

Margie and Officer Archie step aside. I follow my feet down the hall. One step. Two. Three steps. Four. There's mud on the daisy rug Mom made me, an evidence bag on my bed.

"I'm sorry about the mud," Officer Archie says. He grabs up the evidence bag and tucks it away.

One step. Two. Three steps. Closet. I pull down two duffle bags. Margie disappears, comes back with three big suitcases that roll around on wheels. I don't remember them.

I have a lot of books. We pack them up. They fit. I take clothes, my journals, my wannabe iPod and an old laptop Mom bought last year. I leave Tiananmen Square and the brave tank man behind.

There's only one book left—the paperback I'm rereading for the third time—*The Stand* by Stephen King.

"How can you stomach all that horror stuff, Lilybeans?"

"It's about more than that."

"But everyone dies."

"Not everyone. There's Stu and Larry and Joe and Mother Abigail and Tom Cullen and Nick and Frannie. Tons of people left. M-O-O-N, that spells starting over."

The phone in Mom's room rings. Hank. Must be Hank. I hear bees buzzing again, loud in my ears, taking over everything. Then peace.

"Lily?" Margie's saying. She's at my side now. I don't know when she crossed the room. One minute she was at the closet, the next, she's right next to me, like I blinked and she teleported. I'm still holding my book.

"Just about done," I say.

"Where'd you go, kiddo?"

"Again?"

Margie nods. "A few minutes this time. Couldn't move ya, kid." She's trying to make light, but it's no good. The fear is huge in her eyes and her cell phone's clutched tight in her hand.

"Was it like before?" Margie asks. Her voice is feathery in this silent mausoleum, a wisp of sound the dead house won't echo. Nothing is like what it was before, but that's not what she's asking.

"I guess so."

"Do you remember anything?"

I lift *The Stand* to show Margie. "I was having memories about this book."

She nods. "All that time?"

"No, a few seconds I think."

"And then what?"

"Ringing. Mom's phone ringing?"

Margie's face creases. "It didn't ring. What about the bees?"

"They were there. Loud."

"What do you remember after that?"

"You calling my name."

"Anything I can do to help?" Officer Archie says. He's ready for us to go.

Fear dissolves. Margie is Margie again. "Would you help us haul this out?"

"Of course," he says.

"Shall we?" Margie says. She's got one arm held out, sweeping me toward the door. Her other hand is holding tight to her cell phone. We're pretending about the lost minutes. We're pretending she's not thinking about Mack and Darcy.

I look around my empty bedroom and take a deep breath of dog food. My last. "I'm ready."

"We might have to make two trips," Margie says.

"No, it'll fit."

"Your mom always said you knew just how things would fit. Instinctively. Like that dresser." Margie points at the big vanity Mom and I carried up here ourselves. "You could tell that would fit through the door before you brought it home."

"Mom told you that?"

She nods and her eyes are bright now. She's close to saying "Your mom was really proud of you" or something like it.

"I'm ready," I say again before her mouth opens.

We wait in the hotel, not eating much, not swimming in the pool, only sometimes sleeping. We wait for Officer Archie to call and tell us they caught Hank. We don't talk about Grandpa Henry's money again or anything important. I don't tell Margie about Hank at the dog food house. I think seeing Hank with his gun and his paintbrush might get me sent someplace besides Seattle, besides Mack and Darcy's. Maybe the loony bin. We don't talk about the bees either. We're quiet, me and Margie.

Margie's cell phone plays a song. It's not about Hank, I see by her face. It's about Mom. When she hangs up she says words I don't want to hear. "We can lay your mom to rest, Lily."

She touches my arm, keeping me here. "She wanted to be cremated. Did you know that?"

"No," I say. "But it makes sense." Mom didn't like it when people were tricked out of their money—a funeral, her biggest example.

"It's ridiculous—an expensive box to rot in the ground. Money should be spent on the living. The dead don't care."

We decide to spread Mom's ashes in a hidden meadow where she and I spent most of every weekend last summer. Not this summer, though. This summer isn't quite here. Next weekend was supposed to be our first trip up. Five miles in the car, another two on foot. It's quiet there. Peaceful.

"When?" I say.

Margie squints at me. I have to ask in more words so she understands. "When can we take Mom up?"

"It'll be a few days yet. I know you want to get this all put behind you. I know that. I wish I could make it go faster."

Margie doesn't understand. When you want to put things behind, you usually have something in front. There is no front for me. No future.

Pretty soon the tears will start. Pretty soon there'll be a crack and then a flood.

Pretty soon I'll dissolve, disappear, vanish into the ether like the life we had at the dog food house.

"Would you like to say a few words?" Margie's asking. We're standing in the middle of Mom's meadow with wildflowers blooming right up around us, going about their business like Mom didn't die. Purple fades to pink. Yellow into red. Dew on our sneakers. The earth sinking, soft with spring, the sky blue and cloudless.

I'm standing in Mom's meadow. I'm holding the urn that holds her.

"Lily?"

"I love her," I say. I look at the urn. "I love you."

There's a hot tightness in my stomach. Aching behind my eyes. Hollow in my chest where my heart's supposed to be. *Thump-crack, thump-crack.*

"I'm sorry," I whisper. "I'm sorry I didn't answer the phone." It's all I can say because the heat and the ache and the hollow want to come out, to dissolve me. There are worse places to become nothing, but I'm weak, not brave like Mom. After Hank's light went out, when he let in Grandpa Henry's poison, he made sure I knew.

"Your so pathetic, Lily. A weak-willed, mewling little brat."

Margie says a few words too, letting the heat and ache out. She stays Margie, though, and doesn't dissolve. She tells Mom she's sorry for what her brother did, for how things turned out.

We take the lid off the urn, walk around the meadow and spread Mom's ashes. A little for the black-eyed Susans. A lot for the honeysuckle growing up the side of a tree—her favorite. A little more for the dogwood and the bluebells and the cosmos.

Glass into sand. Mom into ashes. Ashes into earth. The earth is small enough. My focus: the earth.

Me and Margie, we sit next to each other in the softness and dew, in the warm sun. We sit down with our living bodies and watch the breeze carry Mom to every corner of her hidden meadow.

"Lilybeans, pull one of those black-eyed-Susans for your hair. Tuck it behind your ear. That's it!" Click. Snap.

"This is a beautiful spot," Margie says.

"Lil, lean against that tree, will you? Grab a honeysuckle flower, hold it under your nose. Good girl." Click. Snap.

"I can see why you and your mom spent so much time here."

"Lily! Did you see the rabbit? We have to get a picture!" Click. Snap.

Margie scoots close, puts her arm around me. "I thought we'd leave for Seattle on Friday. What do you think?"

"What about Hank?"

Margie doesn't say anything for a minute. We listen to the crows complaining in their scratchy voices. We watch the Susans bend their miniature sunflower heads. We feel a soft breeze come through, rustle the long grass. So much quiet.

"Do you hear that, Lily?"

"What?"

"Nothing. It's so silent, so peaceful here. Can you feel it?"

"Sure, Mom, whatever you say."

"There's no yelling. No fighting. Just the wind and the meadow."

"It's nice."

"Yes."

"Are you worried about Hank?" Margie's taken the silver box out of her purse again and she's turning it over in her hands. I see it's etched with little flowers. Very detailed. I think it's maybe a touchstone for Margie.

"No," I say and it's the truth.

Margie's fingers quiet down and she holds the box in one palm.

"What is that?" I ask.

She gestures for me to hold out a hand and sets the little box on my palm. I expect it to be warm, but it's cold. I expect it to be light, but it's heavy.

"I made it. You know what I do for a living?"

I think back to stuff Mom said, to Margie's T-shirt in the hospital. "A metallurgist or something?"

"That's right. This little thing"—she touches one finger to the top of the box—"is a hobby." Margie's whole body sighs. "Metal runs in our veins, kiddo. The little cat your dad made?"

I nod.

"Looks like he couldn't get away from it either. No matter what we did, it all came back to this."

She brushes her fingertips across the box's lid.

"Didn't that make Grandpa Henry happy?" I ask even though I know the answer already. Grandpa Henry owns—owned—a company called Berkenshire Metalworks. The only thing I know about it is that Hank didn't want to install rain gutters or build chain link fences or put up security gates.

Margie shakes her head. "I'm afraid nothing ever did. I stopped trying when I left home."

"Hank too. For a while."

"Yes, Hank too."

"He was happy when he painted, when he made those little animals for me. Not always happy, but better than after he went to work for Grandpa Henry."

"Your mom said he started drinking."

"When I was little. I think he hated his jobs." Every year a different color uniform shirt, but always his name embroidered on the chest. *Hank.* At first, just six-packs of beer disappeared overnight. And then after Grandpa Henry, more than just beer. Big bottles of whiskey gone in a flash and Mom and me seeing a lot of movies on school nights so we weren't home before he passed out.

Margie sees my frowning face, pulls me close and cuts off my breath with her tight hug. "You don't have to worry about that now, Lilybeans."

I think Margie, with her not knowing that Hank wanted to kill me too, believes we'll be safe. I also know if she doesn't think she can protect me, she'll call up Mack and Darcy. Fear and a promise to Mom will make her think of their ranch in the middle of the desert where Hank can't find me. If she knew about his bullets for me, she'd send me today.

I shove these thoughts away, these Mack and Darcy thoughts. I think about Hank's dead-and-cold father instead. "Do we need to bury Grandpa Henry?" I ask.

Margie shakes her head. "He took care of everything and there's no way I'm seeing him laid to rest."

"Okay, I understand."

"Anyone you want to say good-bye to before we go?" Margie's voice tells me she already knows there isn't.

"No."

We wait a little longer, for a whisper, a *good-bye,* to come along.

It doesn't.

On the way back from the meadow, we visit Margie's mom in an old cemetery. She wants to say something, probably tell her what Hank did. I turn my back and wander a little ways while she talks to the ground. I try not to hear what she says, but I catch snippets anyway. "You should have left Dad when we were young, when we had a chance. You knew what he was capable of."

I walk farther away so Margie has privacy, keeping watch for Hank, wondering if he'd be so stupid. So far, there is no Hank. So far, there's only a feeling of him out there with his patient waiting, with his imaginary picture-taking that says *see you later*.

The cemetery is nice. It's one of those old ones with leaning headstones that have grass growing up around them. Big trees cast long shadows across engraved names so you're left bending down to read if you want to know who's buried under your feet. I bend down a few times before Margie's ready to go.

"Are you okay?" she asks.

"Yes," I say.

We walk back toward the road. Margie's rental car sits on a long stretch of asphalt cutting through the old graveyard. A trail right through the dead that leads to somewhere I can't see.

PART II

At fifteen, life had taught me undeniably
that surrender, in its place, was as honorable as
resistance, especially if one had no choice.
- Maya Angelou, *I Know Why The Caged Bird Sings*

Margie keeps her word and we leave for Seattle on Friday. We let Goodwill take the rest of the stuff from the house. It's not much. I have my books, the sweater Mom knitted, my rug, our pictures—everything important.

It's too long a drive, Margie says, so we're flying. It's my first time in an airplane. I'm not nervous. There's no room inside for nerves. All seats taken.

It's a short flight and pretty soon we're walking through the airport, yanking suitcases off the carousel. I'm watching Margie pull on the bag that holds my books when whiskey and paint fill my nose. He's on the other side of the rotating luggage. He's wearing the same jeans with red stains, has the same booze belly hidden underneath the same flannel shirt, same paint and blood-splattered work boots. Margie doesn't notice, probably wouldn't recognize him. Twenty years ago Hank was a kid, in better shape and handsome in the few pictures I saw. Now he's all spindly arms and legs with a skeletal, triangular head and glassy, black eyes. A praying mantis with hands instead of pincers. A praying mantis with a gun.

Mint joins the crowd and the bees start buzzing their broken song. I know what it means, the *buzz-buzz-buzz*. It means silence and peace for a little while. It means nothingness—something I don't mind so much. Not here, though. Here there are too many people, too much bustle. Here there's Margie with her worry.

Someone brushes me where I'm standing at the carousel, brushes me hard because I'm frozen staring at not-Hank or Hank, taking up space and not moving. Both of us watching, not moving, fixed in this here-and-now moment. Margie's voice is next to my ear, but I can't make out the words. The bees are too loud. People are bustling all around and the quiet place is a blink away. Don't go. Don't go. Stay. Please stay.

I can't.

When I come back we're still at the carousel and Margie's standing in front of me. She's not embarrassed even though people are staring. She's scared. Plenty. But not embarrassed. This helps.

"Hi, Aunt Margie."

"Hi, Lilybeans. How ya doin'?"

I look over Margie's shoulder. There's no more Hank or not-Hank across the way, no more mint or whiskey, no paint either. Everything is the way it's supposed to be. Margie glances over her shoulder at where I'm staring.

"I'm okay," I say. "Should we go?"

Her skin is creased between her eyebrows, but she doesn't ask anything. We get the luggage and head to the parking lot.

We're driving away from the airport, through

the city, and I'm remembering when Mom and I came to stay with Margie last summer. I remember the shabby brick wall we're passing now painted bright with a Seahawks logo, how the new paint made the brick look even more worn out. The Seahawk is faded now, a year and a thousand storms gone by.

I remember the Space Needle, the downtown buildings made of glass and brick and metal, towering over a city people say is emerald, but right now is gray. It was sunny when we visited Margie last summer. Now there are no fluffy clouds, no warmth. Everything is dull and dim. Foggy.

I look out my window and see a harbor through the rain drops sliding down the glass. The water out there looks mad, waves crashing one way, waves crashing another way, banging into each other like they've got nothing better to do.

Pretty soon there's a guy on the corner, waving his arms, hollering at an invisible audience. We sit at a red light and I watch him, thinking about the Hank or the not-Hank in the airport, wonder if seeing Hank means I'm crazy or if it means he's come for me already. If it was a not-Hank and I keep seeing him, keep hearing the bees, I might end up on a corner someday, waving my arms, talking to invisible people. Or staring into space, not moving, not being. Or maybe even end up like Hank, raging at a gun when it runs out of bullets. His coming that night, I think it did something to make me empty and crazy—like him.

We're on Magnolia Bridge and Margie's asking me if I remember it from last time. I do, but I say I don't so she'll point out the sites and I don't have to talk. She's explaining how all the close-together boats in the water below us is a yacht club, how people sail on the weekends, even when it rains.

"Don't wait for the sun to come out in Seattle, Lily, or you'll never leave the house." She smiles, points to downtown, to the yacht club, to a park with a lot of foggy trees. "Plenty to do here, but we'll take it slow, okay?"

Pretty soon we stop in front of Margie's apartment building. I remember the patio from last summer, sitting out there in the dark watching downtown and the Space Needle light up. Queen Anne—a fancy neighborhood. There's no white steam into blue sky, no stink, no threadbare couches with pots of gold in the cushions.

It's not long before Margie's unlocking her front door. "What did you think about that big house next door? Pretty elaborate, right?"

I look at Margie, feel my eyebrows wrinkle up. I don't remember the house. "I didn't notice," I say.

Margie looks sad, then nods, then shows me my room.

My new room is where Mom and I stayed. We shared the big bed, talked for hours and planned our new life. I feel a whooshing inside, like my stomach's decided to leave my body. I stand in the doorway, frozen, but not gone.

Margie thinks I'm disappointed. "We'll get you your own stuff soon."

"No need. This is fine." The room is still done up in blues and whites like I remember. It's sterile. It's fine.

"No. We'll go shopping when we're both feeling a little better. I'll donate all this stuff. It's old anyway."

"Okay."

"Get settled and I'll check on you in a bit. I need to make a quick call."

Margie disappears and I go to the bed, run my fingers along the bedspread. Mom sat here while I sat on the floor. She braided my hair, said sweet things.

"You have such beautiful hair, Lilybeans. We don't do this enough. Girlie stuff. We'll do more now, I promise."

I didn't know for sure we were leaving Hank yet. I didn't know, but I sometimes hoped. I sit on the floor now, make a wish to feel her fingers again, want to hear her sweet words, wish I could go back. The ache and the hollow start up, the burning behind my eyes.

I look around the bedroom for a distraction. A canvas bag with all my clothes sits over on the chair that matches the desk in here. It's time to unpack.

I open the bag. A cloud of dog food has followed me all the way to Seattle. I wander through the apartment, holding a T-shirt out in front of me—evidence to show Margie why I need to do laundry.

"Yes, we're both home. She's... quiet." Margie's talking on the phone, pacing the living room, her back to me, moving from one bookcase to the next. This living room was my favorite place when we visited. All four walls are stacked high with her paperbacks, first editions and falling-apart hardbacks. It's a miniature library.

The boxes are new, I think: a copper box big enough to hold one of those old-timey dictionaries before you could look up words online; silver boxes so small you could balance one on the end of a finger; a black box, scratched and shiny, old and new all at the same time—a box trying to be a conundrum; and my favorite, a red box with a bird etched into its lid. There's a box for every shelf on every bookcase. A bazillion touchstones.

Margie's playing with a business card, her thumb bending and unbending one corner. She holds it up against the spine of a thick book. I see

"Mack and Darcy Langhorn" with a Utah number underneath. There's nothing else on it but a red/brown fingerprint in one corner—the corner she's bending and unbending. I think Officer Archie must have given her the card. It's a just-in-case card that lets Margie send me away if I'm too much trouble.

"Not talking much, no." Margie pauses, waits for the other person to speak. "There's something wrong. Like she's broken inside. Her eyes are so distant and she's not the Lilybeans I knew. She was always a quiet kid, but she had this light inside that's not there anymore. And she has these spells where she goes completely silent—" Another pause.

"No, she doesn't do anything. Just freezes. You can't wake her up. It's eerie."

Margie waits, nods at the phone, bends the card, unbends the card.

I turn to go.

I hear "Dissociation?" in Margie's scared voice before I'm back in the blue and white room.

I pull out Mom's old laptop. It takes a long time to wake up. I find an open wireless connection and search "Mack and Darcy Langhorn Utah." I guess it won't hurt to know more since if Margie can't take care of me, it's where I'm going anyway.

Langhorn Ranch: Where All Your Beef And Lamb Needs Are Met With 100% Guar-OWN-teed Satisfaction! Mack and Darcy's pictures are cut out and poking above a wide-angled shot of green pastures—a homemade job with ragged edges around their heads and hands. Mack-Hank's eyes are cold with no understanding. Darcy's eyes are vacant, tired, her hands old before they should be. I click "About Us." It's the same picture, only not cut out. They're in the pasture now and behind them are nestled-down sheep, fluffy white cotton balls with no thought to dying because someone's hungry for lamb stew.

At the bottom of the page there's "click here for Rick's page!" I "click here," get redirected to a page with some random guy leaning against a rickety fence, grinning with a feathery stalk of something sticking out from between yellow teeth—teeth that look like they've been shuffled and rearranged like a deck of cards. He's got one thumb hooked in the front pocket of his jeans. His other arm stretches over the top of the fence. It's not his thumb or his arm or his teeth I care about, though. It's his smile. It's his eyes. He's another Hank. It's more than coldness and not understanding. It's something I don't want to know about. *Rick Mirely—member of the Langhorn team,* the caption under his picture says.

I close the laptop, decide not to think about Rick-the-team-member, his eyes telling me all about what's inside him, or about Mack-Hank and how at the hospital he had no understanding or patience.

Mostly I decide not to think about the nature shows Hank forced me to watch after his light went out, how he said watching animals die on TV would make me stronger, help me face my fears. How he'd change the channel quick when Mom came home and pretend I was crying for a different reason. But Mom knew. Before we left, my light starting going out too. Mine and Mom's, busy flickering because of Hank's choices and Grandpa Henry's poison. We left barely in time and then it didn't matter anyway.

Margie pokes her head in.

"How you doing in here, kiddo?"

"Waiting."

"For me?"

"Yes. I went looking for you, heard you on the

phone."

She looks surprised. "I'm sorry, Lily. I hope that didn't hurt your feelings."

"No."

"I was talking with your new therapist. He wanted to know how you were doing."

"Okay."

"His name is Dr. Pratchett. You'll see him every Thursday starting next week."

"What about your work, my school?"

Margie nods, her eyes on the floor. "It's so close to summer I'm not going to enroll you until next fall." She looks up. "The good news is, you had enough credits to pass your sophomore year."

I didn't, but it's okay.

"As for work, I have to go back next week." She's an important person, Margie. A metallurgist, sure, but a bigwig too. Supervisor, CEO, head honcho. Something.

"I thought you might like to stay here while I'm at work. Kind of a boring summer, but—"

"That sounds good, Aunt Margie. I could read. You have a lot of books."

"That I do. Well, that *we* do. My books are your books now. We'll get some shelves in here for your own collection."

"Okay. Thanks."

She gauges me for a bit, her eyebrows raised, her mouth crooked and undecided. "Dr. Pratchett's asked me not to pester you. Bet you'll be glad of that."

"It's okay."

"He wants you to accept what happened in your own time."

I don't know what Margie's saying.

"Dr. Pratchett says it's important to let the memories in. Little by little. The good and the bad. I told him about your spells."

"Okay." I wait a few seconds so she knows I have a question. "Is it okay if I use your washing machine?"

"Of course." She leads me to a whole room where she's got her washer and dryer.

I spend the next little while doing laundry, getting that dog food smell out of my clothes. Between loads, I go back to the blue and white bedroom and sit on the bed or in a chair by the window. I don't open the laptop again. I decide Hank's small bullet is better than Mack and Darcy's ranch, better than Rick-the-team-member with that strange light in his eyes.

When there's no smell left, I go into the living room. Margie's sitting on the couch. She puts down the book she's reading and smiles.

"How will I get there?" I say.

She squints her eyes and shakes her head. I haven't used enough words again.

"How will I get there on Thursdays? To Dr. Paget's?"

"Dr. Pratchett's. I'll drop you off and pick you up. Tomorrow we'll go on the bus and I'll show you the route just in case I get stuck at work one day. Does that sound okay to you?" She looks worried about the bus idea, like just saying it out loud will make it come true.

"Sounds good."

"I have to take classes starting next week so the state knows I can take good care of you. I'll be gone on Wednesday evenings."

"I'm sorry for all the fuss."

"No fuss," Margie says. She crosses to me, brushes my bangs back. "No fuss at all."

The next morning Margie takes me on the bus to Dr. Pratchett's building. It's a straightforward route, no transferring. I'll find it if I need to.

"This is just in case I get stuck at work, Lil. My plan is to take you every week."

"Okay."

The building is a big glass one with dancing fountains out front. Yards of concrete lead up to heavy glass doors. There's a fond smile on Margie's face. "I saw Dr. Pratchett for awhile after I moved here. He helped me a lot."

I figure Margie saw Dr. Pratchett for stuff Grandpa Henry said. Probably he made her light flicker too. There's no flickering anymore, though. Margie's light is strong and warm—a happy light I don't mind being around.

Margie nudges me. "He'll help you too. I just know it."

"Okay."

"Feel like heading to my favorite bookstore?"

"Yes."

Margie looks happy. "Thought that might cheer you up."

I think I smile, but by the look on Margie's face, it's something else. She puts her arm around me and guides me back to the bus stop. I wonder if I've forgotten how to smile, how to feel something besides nothing.

We ride for a little while before we stop at a bookstore with a neon cat on its sign. I know right off I'm going to like this place. The front picture window holds a big display of books and a tabby cat, orange-and-white striped, stretched out on a cushy bed, watching the world go by. A bell jingles over the door when we open it. The cat raises his head, but doesn't get up. He's watching me with yellow eyes and I can't help but ignore the stacks of books and head right to his perch.

Pretty soon I'm leaning into the display window, giving the tabby's head a stroke.

"His name's Cheetah."

I glance over to see a woman with long white-gray hair and a worn face. Happiness and intelligence dance in her eyes and her smile is easy.

"He's sweet," I say. By now Cheetah's getting up off his bed so he can have a more thorough pet. He looks ready to jump into my arms.

"Careful, he'll decide to go home with you."

"That'd be okay, huh, boy?" I give his silky ears a good rub and turn back to Margie.

Her eyes are full, her mouth turned up. "I think he likes you," she says, pointing over my shoulder.

I look and Cheetah's stretched as far toward me as he can get, his paw just brushing Mom's sweater. I crouch down and he climbs onto my bent legs. The lady with the worn face lets out a big laugh. "Well, I guess you've been claimed." She steps behind the front counter and I see now she's the owner of the shop.

I sit down on the floor and let Cheetah cuddle in. "You go ahead, Aunt Margie. I'll stay here a little while."

Margie smiles and nods. "Okay, kiddo. I'll check on you in a few." She wanders into the shop while I stroke Cheetah, accept his kisses on my cheek. With this orange fur ball on my lap, I feel a little something inside. It's not a big something, not anything earth-shattering. A quiet something that made Margie smile. Cheetah feels like a tether. He makes me want to ignore the buzzing, to keep out of the quiet place, to stay here for a little while.

"Never seen him do that with someone so soon. You've got the touch," the store owner says from her spot behind the counter.

"Okay."

Her laugh, loud and good-natured, bounces off the books around me. It's not like Mom's soft tinkling laugh, but still nice. She disappears into a room I haven't noticed until now—her office, I think.

Cheetah's busy purring and kneading my leg with sharp claws when I hear the bell over the door jingle. Paint-splattered work boots stop in front of me. Hank. I keep my eyes on Cheetah, remembering not-Hank at the airport, at the dog food house. This will be a not-Hank too, I tell myself.

"That's a cute kitty you've got there, Beans."

I look up slowly. My eyes are his eyes. He's not wearing flannel, but a black button-down shirt instead, different jeans, no stains, same crazy smile.

"Leave me alone," I say. I don't expect the

tremble in my voice or my words. I want him to disappear like the others, disappear because he's not really here.

He laughs his soft, mad laugh and slowly lowers himself to the floor. He sits cross-legged like me, our knees almost touching. Today he doesn't smell like anything and I wonder where his whiskey's gone, where he's stashed the mints he's always chewing to cover up his boozy breath. "Sorry, kiddo. We've got some talking to do."

I look around the shop. We're alone. It doesn't matter. I can't tell Aunt Margie Hank's here. If he's in Seattle, he'll hurt Margie. If he isn't and I'm crazy, it's Mack and Darcy's for me. Or the loony bin.

"Could we talk later maybe?"

"Where's my sister?" He says the word like it tastes bad in his mouth, like Margie being his sister makes him feel sick.

My neck cracks when I shake my head side-to-side. "Leave Aunt Margie alone." I plead with my voice, with my eyes.

Hank laughs again and reaches across to stroke Cheetah's head. His laugh reminds me of when he would call at night to say bad things about Mom, make fun of us for trying to be on our own. I think about the phone ringing the night he came with his bullets. Sometimes I forget my not answering the phone is why he pounded on the door, came in, took Mom.

"It was my fault," I say.

Hank stops stroking Cheetah's head and looks at me. "What?"

"What you did. It was my fault. Because I didn't answer the phone."

His head tilts to the side. He studies me and I study him. Finally, his eyes roll like he's listening to something. I'm wondering if Hank's hearing bees too when he says, "Not quite time yet." His hands are on his knees and I notice little flecks of paint—a spot of red, a lot of white, some silver.

"Not time for what?" I ask even though I don't think I want to know.

His eyes roll to mine again. Hurt to rage. Blink. Rage to hurt. "You know that bastard talks to me more now than when he was alive?" Hank says this like he's asking what I think of the gray clouds outside. Casual-like, Hank tells me he's hearing Grandpa Henry's voice.

Hank gets up and walks over to the door. His head is bowed, his lips moving and not moving. "When it's time, we'll go to my father's house. We'll go back to where it started and finish it. That should make the old bastard happy." He turns to me and smiles in a sad, decided way. His sad, decided smile makes me jump a little inside, makes a bee start knocking around inside my head. "When it's time I'll come back for you. You have fun with Margie 'til then, okay? She was a good sister when we were growing up. Good and kind." He gives me a look like he wants to say more, then his eyes cloud over and go flat with no light. "Good and kind until she left. Like your mother. Like you." He nods at me once. "You go ahead and tell Margie about our little chat if you want. Then she can come along with us when it's time." He opens the door. "See ya soon, Beans."

The shop owner comes out of her office, muttering under her breath. She smiles at me and at Cheetah asleep in my lap. "Doing okay?"

I nod, but keep staring at her. The question is big in me, pushing to get out.

"You sure?" she asks, her voice all laughter and light.

"Did you hear the door?" I point to the bell that jingles when someone comes in for all their new and used book needs.

She looks around. "I didn't, but I was on the phone. Was someone bothering you? Sometimes we get unusual folk in here."

I shake my head right away and focus on Cheetah. "No, it's okay. I just thought I heard the bell, but then I didn't see anyone."

"Ah. Happens now and then if the wind kicks up," she says. "Or…" She grins at me, grins big and her eyes sparkle. "Sometimes there's a ghost likes to wander these dusty cases. What do you think about that?"

A ghost. "I think you're right," I say.

I put Cheetah back on his perch and stand up, brushing orange and white fur off my clothes. Fine, silky hairs float in the sunshine streaming through the front windows.

"Are you okay?" The store lady's come over without me noticing and is standing a few feet away.

I look into the woman's kind eyes and hope she doesn't see how empty I am. "Cheetah is a great cat."

She reaches into the window and pats the orange tabby on the head. He's too busy getting ready for a snooze to notice her. "He's a special boy. Been here, oh 'bout, five years now."

"He lives in the store?"

"Along with three others." She cocks a thumb over her shoulder toward the books piled up on tables and in bookcases. "All sleeping the afternoon away if today's no different than any other. Think they'd snooze right through an earthquake if it was up to them." She laughs and shakes her head. Her hair tumbles around her, a silver waterfall shining in the overhead lights. Her face is transformed by her smile and I remember Mom again, how her smile was like that—all light and happiness before

Hank started installing rain gutters, and then again after we left, how it lit her entire being right up and anyone standing near her.

Margie's heading down one of the aisles toward the front of the store. "Please don't tell my aunt about the ghost, okay?" I roll my eyes. "She had a bad experience and ghosts scare her." The tremble in my voice is gone, replaced by a casualness I don't feel. I see I'm going to become a good liar.

The shop owner stares at me for another few seconds while Margie walks and reads and doesn't pay attention to where she's going. "Sure thing." She doesn't say anything else, but I see she'll keep her word.

"Thank you."

I meet Margie at the front counter.

"How you doing, Lilybeans?"

"Fine," I say. "You ready to go?"

"Anytime you are." She looks at my empty hands. "Didn't find anything?"

"Not this time."

The shop lady doesn't mention ghosts or my weirdness to Margie and I nod at her again before we go—a silent thank you for a silent gift. We leave after I give Cheetah a good-bye pat. He's wearing a sulky expression when we walk past the front window.

Hank's expression isn't sulky where he's standing across the street with his cup of steaming coffee. Hank's expression is stony. Decided. He raises his hand not holding the coffee, thumb and index finger in an L, taking a pretend picture.

See you later.

It's Thursday and today's focus is easy: get to Dr. Pratchett's by one o'clock. Margie's at work now. She'll honk out front when she picks me up. I'll have to listen and be ready.

All morning I read in a chair Margie's got arranged next to the patio doors. It's big enough for two people or for one to fold her legs up, cozy like. The sun warms it every day it's not cloudy. Today it's sunny and the chair is toasty. I'm drowsy from the warmth and from not sleeping too well at night. I keep reading, though. I'm getting to the end of *The Stand*, to the big showdown.

A bell dings softly in the apartment. I've drowsed off, my book on the floor now, pages folded, mashed under the weight of a thousand brethren. I pick it up and put it on the table next to me, then blink hard to clear my foggy brain. Margie's set an alarm for me to get ready for Dr.

Pratchett's. I have thirty minutes until she's supposed to honk. Margie said this morning it might be a good idea I pull a brush through my hair before I go.

The bell is a timer on the oven. I click it off and head back to the blue and white bedroom.

I stop too fast in the hallway, feet skidding on the hardwood floor. Hank's on the bed where Mom sat cross-legged to braid my hair. Everything in me jumps and I want to grab him and make him move from where Mom sat. He's busy infecting this place with his whiskey and paint, his mints, busy polluting the air and twisting memories.

We stare at each other and pretty soon the bees start up, buzzing their broken pattern in my brain. Hank's eyes are glassy with their flat light, his gaze steady on me. He doesn't blink, doesn't move, just sits cross-legged like he did at the bookstore, only now he's wearing his flannel again and his jeans with their dark stains.

"What do you want?"

He doesn't say anything.

I'm watching my feet now, how they shuffle back and forth, how they don't want to run from Hank-the-murderer. They're content right where they are, my feet. I think they know more than my head, so I listen to them instead of the bees starting to knock around inside my skull. *Buzz-buzz-buzz,* making me believe the quiet place will be better than Hank sitting in this blue and white bedroom. This room where Mom and I, we talked about the way things were at home, how Hank had already driven away everyone we knew.

"What ever happened to your friend Heather?"

I'm relaxed, sleepy from how good Mom's fingers feel braiding my hair, so I don't think before I speak. "Dad told her she was too fat to be my friend."

Mom's fingers still and then pull too hard.

"Ouch!"

She's gentle again, apologizing for all the yanking. "And Tara?"

I don't say anything, don't want to get my hair pulled again.

"Tell me, Lilybeans."

"Dad said she was too lazy."

"Wasn't she on the girl's basketball team?"

"And volleyball and soccer."

"Why didn't you tell me any of this?"

I shrug, not wanting to put more stress on Mom than she already has. She's finishing up the braid, though, and pretty soon she'll be turning me around so she can see what's in my eyes. I might as well tell her and get it all out. "Because you had enough with him changing so much, saying all those things about you. Yelling like you were on the moon."

Mom finishes my hair without saying anything else and pulls me up to sit next to her on the blue and white bed. "From now on, you tell me everything, okay? Everything."

I nod.

She tucks a stray hair behind my ear and kisses my cheek. "I'm sorry this last year has been so hard."

I run my fingers along the silky bedspread. I was never a super chatty kid, but in the last year, I haven't been able to string ten words together at a time. All my friends have been driven away by Hank's drinking and his meanness. Mom and me, our lives about school and work and home and nothing else. Hank with his suffocating control, his crazy belief we were doing bad things. Mom and me, our lives about nothing but Hank's growing rage.

With Hank sitting on the blue and white bed and these memories about Mom, the bees get so loud I can't ignore them anymore. I go where it's quiet.

&

The cell phone Margie gave me is playing a tune from where I left it in the living room. Hank's gone, vanished from the bedroom. I'm still in the hall, my smart feet tired from standing. I get to the cell phone and pick it up in time.

"Hello?" I say.

"Hi, Lily. Are you okay?" Margie says.

"I'm okay."

"This is my third time trying you. Whatcha up to?"

"Looking out the window. Waiting for your honk."

"How are you? Did you eat?"

"I fell asleep."

"Sleep is good, but you have to eat too."

"I know. I'm sorry."

"It's okay. We'll get you something on the way home. I'm a few minutes away."

"Okay."

"See you in a bit."

"Okay."

I don't mention Hank with his whiskey smell, his being in the blue and white bedroom and then disappearing, not leaving so much as a wrinkle on the bedspread. A not-Hank after all is what I think. A not-Hank with his silence, his clothes that show what he did to Mom, his smelling like he did that night. I think about him at the bookstore, in the blue and white bedroom, wonder if they're all not-Hanks and I'm maybe closer to the loony bin than I thought.

We get to Dr. Pratchett's office on time. "Remember, Lilybeans, fifteenth floor, number 1504. It's on that post-it in your pocket too. Tell Dr. Pratchett hello from me, okay?"

"Okay, Aunt Margie. See you in awhile."

I get out of Margie's car where the bus stop is. There's no bus now—just us. I walk across the field of concrete. Thin clouds make everything gray now, dim the sky, the trees.

I find the elevator and ride up by myself. Fifteenth floor, number 1504. I open a door, see there's another door too, into the therapy office I guess. I'm sitting in a chair in the waiting room, waiting. None of the magazines look good, so I just sit and try to figure out my next focus. *Finish* The Stand. It's a good one and reminds me of Margie's toasty chair.

A few minutes or a few hours later, the knob to the inner office twists. A man who has to duck through the doorway comes into the waiting room. He's got dark and light gray hair, all mixed up like concrete that's dry in some spots, wet in others. He wears his glasses pulled down on his nose. "Lily?" he says over them.

I nod and stand up.

"It's nice to meet you," he says and holds out a hand for me to shake. I do. "I'm Dr. Pratchett. Would you like to come in?"

"Okay."

He leads the way into a dimly-lit office full of expensive furniture. There's a lot of leather in here, including the top of his desk. It smells nice—spicy, like Christmas. He has enormous bookshelves and I walk right over to them, trail my fingers down the spines of books I've never heard of. Some look like first editions and I drop my hand to my side. "Sorry," I say.

"No need. Go ahead and touch anything you like. Are you a reader?"

I glance over my shoulder at Dr. Pratchett where he's leaning against his desk. "You could say that."

He nods. He's got a moustache I'm just noticing. It matches his hair—dry and wet concrete. "Today I thought we could get to know each other a little, make sure you feel comfortable working with me."

"Okay."

"If you decide you'd like to see someone else, I have some referrals ready for you. Sound good?"

"Yes."

"One more thing, Lily. Whether you decide to work with me or someone else, Margie will be privy to everything we discuss here if she decides she wants to know. Sometimes, parents or guardians don't ask, but sometimes they do. How do you feel about that?"

I turn back to the books and keep going. "Fine," I say. I tell myself to remember Dr. Pratchett's words, to not mention Hank at the airport, Hank in the bookstore, Hank in the blue and white bedroom—the not-Hanks that will get me sent to the loony bin or to Mack and Darcy's.

Dr. Pratchett's got bookcases on every wall. I speed up my investigation, skipping over big sections. "What's this one about?" I ask. The spine is stamped *DSM-5*.

"That one helps me decide how I can best help people."

"It helps you diagnose," I say.

Dr. Pratchett looks surprised. "Yes."

"Helps you label people."

"Well…" He shifts to lean against his other leg.

"Have you labeled me?" I ask.

"No, Lily. I don't know you." He laughs at his own joke.

"I heard Margie on the phone."

"With me?"

"Yes."

"Do you have questions about what was said?"

"Dissociation?"

Dr. Pratchett nods. "Do you know what that is?"

"No."

"Margie said you go very quiet sometimes."

"Inside."

"Inside?"

I tap my chest. "In here it's hollow. There's room for me."

Dr. Pratchett's head tips. "Can you tell me more about that?"

I shrug and turn back to the books—old friends I've never met before.

"Do you think about anything when you go inside?"

"It's quiet. Nothing to think about."

"Does it scare you when it happens?"

"No."

"It doesn't scare you to lose time?"

"No. It scares Margie."

"Yes."

"I don't want to scare her."

"You love her very much."

I tap my chest again. "No room."

"For love?"

Nod.

"What is there room for, Lily?"

Shrug.

"Is there room for memories?"

"Sometimes."

"What happens when the memories surface?"

"The hollow gets bigger."

Dr. Pratchett thinks on this awhile. "When you go quiet and you don't think about anything, are you aware?"

"No."

"So you don't know you've been gone until you come out?"

"Yes."

I hear Dr. Pratchett shift while I run a finger down the engraved spine of an old book—*The Grapes of Wrath,* one I had to read for English last semester. About poor people trying not to be poor anymore, about people dying because they were poor, about the haves and the have-nots. About Hank working for Grandpa Henry's money and me and Mom in our dog food house.

"Dissociation is a common response to trauma, Lily."

"Okay." I wonder if Dr. Pratchett would say the same about Hank on the blue and white bed, stinking up Margie's apartment with his whiskey and paint, his mint. *Not-Hanks are a common response to trauma, Lily.* Somehow I don't think so.

"Sometimes medication is used as part of a treatment plan—"

"No pills," I say.

"It's not my first choice either. I'd like to see how we do in our sessions first."

I brush my fingers along the base of a trophy. "Nice trophy."

"I'm into sailing. What do you like to do?"

I walk to the chair I think I'm supposed to sit in. I sit. There's a couch too, but I don't feel like laying down, like being a cliché. "Reading," I say.

Dr. Pratchett smiles. "I gathered that. What else?"

I think for a minute, but not outside my small focus. "I don't mind riding the bus here. Seattle is pretty."

Dr. Pratchett sits in a matching leather chair facing the one I'm in. He crosses one leg over another and folds his clasped hands around his knee. I see argyle socks inside dress shoes. He doesn't have a notebook or a pen.

"Aren't you going to write anything down?"

"Not while we're talking. I'll make some notes after you leave."

"So you can remember me if I come back next week?"

His eyes crinkle at the corners. "I think I'd remember you if I didn't take a single note."

"Okay."

Dr. Pratchett leans back in his chair and the leather makes a soft scrunching sound. "What would you like to talk about, Lily?"

"Well, maybe you could point me to some good bookstores?"

"I can do that, certainly. I thought you might also want to tell me a little about yourself. You like to read and you like to ride the bus around the city—"

"I've only taken it from my aunt's apartment to here. Once."

"Well, that's a very good start. What else do you like?"

I let my mind wander for just a minute back to before. It's a narrow path of memories that feels okay. I see an orange fur ball in my lap and feel wet kisses on my cheek. "Animals," I say. "I like animals."

"Do you have a favorite?"

"Cats. I've always wanted one."

"Do you think your Aunt Margie would allow you to have a cat?"

I go cold all over and start to shake.

"Lily, are you okay?"

Everything's all caught up in my throat. I can't talk. I hold out my hand, asking Dr. Pratchett to wait with anymore questions. He nods, moves to the edge of his chair and waits with his face creased up, with his eyes not blinking.

I let my body shake for awhile longer. I think about *The Stand,* only *The Stand,* not the fact that Mom and I were going to pick out a cat at the humane society right after school was done for the year—a reward for my good grades, a new addition to our family. Two plus one. Now just one.

"Has it been an hour yet?" I ask in a barely-there voice.

Dr. Pratchett frowns a little and looks at his watch. "Not quite. Can you tell me what just happened, Lily?"

"I'm sorry."

"No reason to be sorry. Would you like to talk about it?"

I shake my head. "It's not a good idea right now."

"That's just fine. We'll take it slow. Do one thing

for me?"

"I'll try."

Dr. Pratchett's smile is warm, comforting. "Good. Before giving it any thought, toss out a single word you would use to describe how you're feeling right now. Just one word. Right off the top of your head."

"Tin."

"Tin?"

"Hollow. A tin girl. Yes."

"Can you tell me why?"

"There's nothing left."

"Nothing at all?"

I shake my head. He doesn't believe me, but he doesn't push either. If he knew I'd seen not-Hank in Seattle, he'd believe me. Normal people get scared when they think they're going crazy. It's when there's nothing left inside that a person can *not* be afraid.

The clock on Dr. Pratchett's desk says it's time to go. I stand up.

He looks at me for a minute before he stands too. "Are you sure you're okay to go by yourself?"

I make the corners of my mouth turn up, but then remember Margie's expression when I tried before and press my lips back together. "Yes, I'm okay. Margie's waiting in her car downstairs. I'll go straight there."

He holds his hand out and says, "It was very nice meeting you, Lily. How do you feel about coming back next week?"

I watch Dr. Pratchett for a minute. There's no pity in his eyes, only kindness and concern. I wonder if maybe he can help me stop seeing Hank and hearing the bees. Maybe Dr. Pratchett can help me not go crazy all the way. His office full of leather furniture, the spicy-like-Christmas smell, these help me decide. I guess if I have to see a doctor he's a pretty good one.

"Okay," I say and shake his hand.

Dr. Pratchett looks pleased and gives me a card with his number on it, says call him anytime I need to, then shows me a secret door that looks like a wall. It leads out into a hallway doubling back on his front entrance. I guess this is so his crazies don't run into each other in the waiting room. I wonder if he thinks we'll compare notes.

I make the turn, zoom past Dr. Pratchett's office again and get to the elevator. Shiny metal doors distort my too-pale face, twisting it into something not quite right. There are sharp cheekbones where soft fullness was before, my brown-black eyes made bigger by the paleness that surrounds, by the pounds I've lost from not eating, not sleeping, keeping watch. My lips are white and pressed tight to keep it all inside—the buzzing and the memory of that night. With all the paleness, with the hollow and nothing left, with Mack and Darcy just around the corner, or the psych ward if I keep seeing not-Hanks, I am nothing but a living ghost.

A bee starts up. Just one. A baby learning to fly, knocking around in my head, letting me know the quiet wants to come. Pretty soon the bee wants to invite friends, to get the buzzing going full blast so I can't ignore it.

I look at the lit-up number circle above the elevator so I don't have to see my living ghost face, so I can try not to hear the buzzing. The elevator is stuck on the thirtieth floor when I hear Dr. Pratchett's office door squeak open down the hall. I step forward fast and flatten my back against the elevator's cold steel. He wouldn't hear the bees, but he'd know by my face, tell Margie, say I need to be near people who can look after me better.

The door squeaks closed again and I peek down the hall to make sure. Shut tight. I lean against the elevator again, its chill seeping through Mom's sweater and into my body.

I'm thinking about taking the stairs when the elevator doors finally open behind me. I stumble backward, sit down hard and lose my breath.

Someone's laughing and leaning over me. "Are you okay?" he asks.

He's beautiful and smiles like he doesn't know there's ever been anything but happiness in the world. He's taller than I am and his eyes are green and they're full to the brim with light and so much life. He's a good tether, this boy with the dancing eyes, the wide, easy smile. He makes the knocking-around bees go for now.

"Are you sure you're okay?" he asks again as I get back on my clumsy feet. His voice is deep like a man's, but I think he's around my age.

"Yes," I say.

He holds out a hand for me to shake. "I'm Nick Anders."

His skin is a light cocoa color and reminds me of chocolate chips melted in a pot on the stove. I think his parents must be black and white—Yin and Yang to make a beautiful boy with brown skin and light eyes. His hand is soft and warm and tingly with little sparks I don't expect. "Like Nick Andros."

"Who?"

I shake my head. "Fictional character. I'm Lily Berkenshire."

"Do you live in the building?"

"People live in this building?"

Nick tilts his head. "Yes," he says. "You don't?"

"No."

"Are you visiting someone?"

"I'm visiting a doctor who wants to talk about cats and tin." I glance away from Nick's big smile, wondering why these words have left my mouth.

"Sounds like the start of a great book," he says.

I feel the corners of my mouth pull up a little on their own. He doesn't look like Margie did when I tried to smile before, so I think this time I did okay.

"Are you all right?" Nick asks.

"Yes, why?"

He rolls his eyes and smiles even wider. "Well, you aren't shy, for one."

"Something's wrong with not being shy?"

"No, it's just the way you're looking at me."

"How's that?"

"Like you're trying to memorize my face."

I think he's probably right. His smile would make Margie happy, would tell her everything is okay. Maybe if I smile like Nick she'd feel better. Besides, something in his smile holds my attention, keeping me tethered and the bees far away.

"Every girl you meet is shy?"

Nick clears his throat, looks up at the elevator ceiling and taps his chin with an index finger like he's got some long hard thinking to do before he can answer my question. He's opening his mouth, his grin turning lopsided—a smartass grin, I think—when there's a ding and the elevator doors slide open again. A bouncy blonde gets on, stands facing me, then gives me the head-to-toe sweep. Her face pinches up like she's smelling something bad. I'm used to it from my old school and have to push down the impulse to lift my arm and take a big whiff of my sweater to see if that dog food smell didn't all wash out. I stop myself until the elevator doors close, then sniff the cuff of my sleeve.

She glances at Nick, does a double-take, then slides up next to him. She stands close, her arm touching his. "Oh hi, Nicky. Where you going?" Her voice is all melted butter and fake shyness. I think Nick with his beautiful face and dancing eyes probably has a lot of girls go gooey like this.

He leans away, avoiding the blonde's eyes. "Hey, Tiffany. Out and about. You?"

Tiffany starts coiling thick strands of dyed blond hair around one finger. She glances at the floor, at the walls, back to Nick. She pouts and then smiles, like she can't decide which expression is cuter. "To my sister's. She's having a baby in a month and needs help this afternoon." She pulls her hands behind her back and swivels the toes of one foot against the floor. She's wearing high heels that have a strap made of hopefully fake leopard skin. It covers all but her pink toenails. "You wouldn't happen to know how to put together a crib, would you?"

Nick shakes his head fast. "Sorry, I'm no good with tools."

We reach the lobby with a stop so smooth I

don't know we're there until the doors sweep open. I start to move toward them, but I can't get past Tiffany. She's little, but she fills the space up with her glowering and flirting. She ignores me, staring up at Nick through long painted eyelashes, blinking slowly like she's sleepy. "Sure you don't want to come?"

Nick shifts uncomfortably and crosses his arms so he's not touching her anymore. "Sorry. Have fun with your sister, though."

Tiffany squints her eyes and it's easy to see Nick's made her mad. She's not used to not getting her way. "Okay, no problem. Maybe I'll catch you later." Her voice is tight, deep—no more lightness, no more flirting.

Nick smiles politely. "Okay, see you later."

Tiffany's held us up getting off the elevator and the people in the lobby waiting to get on. She doesn't seem to care. She saunters out like no one's there, like she's the only one in the world, her hips swaying back and forth in a tight skirt that doesn't look all that useful for putting together baby furniture. Nick holds his arm out, inviting me to go next. I step out and don't sway my hips at all. I think if I do my jeans will fall down.

I walk past the guard sitting at the front desk and through the first set of double glass doors before I realize Nick's right next to me. I glance up and he's smiling down at me.

"You don't like people holding doors for you?" he says. That's when I realize he's tried to get out in front of me.

"I can open doors," I say. I prove it with the next set of heavy glass. I hold it for him.

He gets an even bigger smile going. "You ever consider an illustrious career in the growing field of door management?" His eyes are almost translucent in the bright afternoon. There are no more gray clouds dimming everything. It's all sunshine and heat and summer blue again, which for sure feels better than the cold steel of the elevator doors.

"I guess that wouldn't be so bad," I say.

He laughs. "Lily Berkenshire, Door Manager. It has a ring."

I glance at this boy, this smiling, happy boy, and see something I didn't notice before. Something familiar. "I've been called worse."

Nick laughs because he thinks it's a joke. "Why'd you smell your sweater when Tiffany looked at you?"

"I used to live next to a dog food factory."

Nick's face is one big question.

"The smell got into my clothes, into everything."

"Where was that?"

"Salt Lake City."

"You live in Utah?"

"No. Not anymore."

"Then why would you still smell like dog food?"

I shrug. "She gave me a funny look. I thought she might have smelled it."

"Oh." He grins. "You want to know why she made that face? And why she ignored you?"

"Okay." We've walked over to the big fountains out in front of the building, so Nick has to talk a little louder because the water's shooting up, splashing back down. It's reflected in the windows, all that glass alive with dancing water. Not splintered glass, not glass hoping for wholeness. Whole on its own.

"It bothers Tiffany when she meets someone prettier than her."

I look at Nick and feel my head tip to the side. I try to see if he's making fun of me, but there's only his smile. And now his easy laugh.

"You don't believe me?"

I see my pasty face distorted in the elevator doors again. I don't believe him, but I don't say so. Nick Anders, happiness on his face for the world to see—he's a good tether. Like Cheetah. I decide I don't want to say he's wrong in case he makes up his mind to go away.

Nick watches me for a little while. I watch him for a little while. "So you live in the city now?" he says.

"With my aunt. Queen Anne?"

"Your Aunt's Queen Anne?" He bows and his hair spills onto his forehead. When he stands he combs through it, making it stand on end again. "I had no idea I was in the presence of royalty."

I don't get Nick's joke at first, but then I do and give him a look that lets him know it was pretty lame.

He just laughs again. "Queen Anne's a nice area," he says, then gives me the once over. "You don't dress like most people up there."

"My mom made me this sweater," I say because I'm not sure what he means.

"It's a nice sweater. Where's your mom?"

I start coughing, double over, try not to choke to death in front of the dancing water. My breath is all caught up in my lungs. My focus is too big. I narrow it, narrow it. *Finish* The Stand. I'll be left an empty husk, a breathless nothing if I can't narrow it. I pluck a loose thread from my sweater. Threads are narrow enough. My thread: *finish* The Stand.

"You okay?" Nick asks. He's worried and busy patting the air above my back as I bend away from him.

"I'm okay," I say. "I need to get to my aunt's."

I focus on walking to the curb. First, I make my feet move three steps. Then I make them move three more. Nick interrupts.

"Are you okay, Lily?" he asks again, like I lied the first time.

I did.

"I am not okay," I say because I'm not. "I am not okay and I don't want to talk about my mom."

"Of course. I'm sorry." Nick watches me closely. He's like Margie when she's deciding if she should push. Finally he puffs a big breath out and lets the words he wants to say go with it. "What are you doing now?"

"Walking."

He laughs a little through the concern, through the guilt that he's why I almost choked to death in front of the dancing fountains. "I mean, are you headed home?"

Nod. "To Aunt Margie's."

"Would you like to go to Pike's Place with me?"

I stop walking. "Why?"

"Well, I'm headed down there and it's a nice day and I thought you might want to come with." He waves one arm around like he's a tour guide. "I could show you our fair emerald city, starting with Pike's where you can, you know, buy a fish or whatever."

"Do I seem like I need a fish?"

"Everyone should totally have a fish of their own."

I think about walking around with Nick-the-stranger, all the people, the bees coming along anytime they feel like it, making me head on into the quiet like there aren't better places to be. "Thank you," I say. "I'd rather not today."

Nick looks surprised, like no one's ever refused his company before. "Do you think I could have your number?" He shuffles his feet and waves one hand around. "Just in case I want to send you a fish or something."

"I don't know it." Margie thinks I've memorized

her home number and my new cell number. I tried, but there's no room inside for numbers.

"Will you be back next week?" he asks.

"Yes."

"Can I meet you right here at say—" He looks at his watch. "Two o'clock?"

"I'll have to see what kind of day it is. I can't say for sure."

"What kind of day?"

"Yes." I spy Margie driving down the road and take three more steps. "Nice meeting you," I mumble because I don't know what else to say.

Margie pulls up and I climb in. Nick is still standing there and he's got a big grin on his face. I wonder if he's like the boys in my old school who laughed at me.

It used to matter, the laughing.

It doesn't anymore.

Days go by like they're minutes, like they're seconds. I read and I only think about the very next thing I have to do. Get out of bed. Take a shower. Eat breakfast. Watch for Hank. Listen for the bees. Answer the phone.

I feel a tug at the first ring, but don't disappear. It's not like our old phone—loud and shrill. Margie's phone is quiet, newer. Fancy.

"Hello?"

"Is this Lily Berkenshire?" The voice is familiar, but I can't place it.

"Yes it is."

"Lily, this is Officer Archie. Do you remember me?"

I see hair that won't shine in the sun, soft eyes, a nice smile. "Yes, I remember."

"I'm calling to see how you are."

"I'm doing okay. How are you?"

He pauses, then laughs a little. "Well, I'm fine, thank you."

There's a long silence that's probably awkward. I wonder if he's going to tell me they've found Hank, found him in Seattle with white and orange cat hairs on his black shirt.

"In our investigation we found something. A letter."

The knot in my chest pounds like it hasn't in awhile. "A letter?"

"Yes, from your mother."

My hands shake so bad the phone knocks me in the head. *Whack.* "To who?" *Whack. Whack.*

"To you, kiddo."

I wait for him to say more. He doesn't. "Did you open it?"

"We had to. I'm sorry. We thought it might be from your father, that it might offer a clue as to where he is."

"Hank," I say. Not my father anymore.

Officer Archie breathes into the phone. "Hank. Yes," he says. His voice understands.

"What–?" I clear my throat, count to five. *Whack. Whack.* "What does it say?"

"I thought I might send it to you. And then you can read it privately?"

I think about this for a long, silent moment. I'm not sure I can wait the two or three days it will take.

"I'll overnight it. It'll be there tomorrow, late morning?" Officer Archie says like he's read my mind.

"Yes, please, that would be great. I have some money—"

"No, that's okay. It's just a few bucks. I'm glad to do it."

"Okay, thank you."

Officer Archie waits a minute. "Lily, I wish I had better news for you. We still have no idea where Hank's gone."

My voice doesn't want to work. "Okay," I croak out anyway.

"I'm sure we'll catch him soon." Officer Archie thinks I'm scared, afraid Hank won't pay for what he did.

"Okay, Officer Archie. Thank you for calling."

"Okay, kiddo. Bye now."

I decide not to think about the letter. It's a big thread, the letter. It's bigger than I can do without disappearing. I don't want Margie to come home and find me gone. I look outside and see it's a beautiful day, decide to venture onto Margie's patio. It's private, quiet. I can't see the street. The street can't see me.

Margie's got some nice furniture out here. I lay down in a cushy chaise lounge and look up at the sky. Whoever said it rained all the time in Seattle never visited during the summer. Margie's got a nice patio, made for grilling and entertaining. I lay my head back, let the heat and sun make me forget.

They make me remember instead.

Mom's prepping dinner in the kitchen—her famous burgers. She flattens them out so they're big patties and soaks them in some kind of booze, brandy or scotch or something. The smell reminds me of Dad, but not for long. She washes what's left down the drain and then it's time for the grill. We head out to the patio.

"Here's a good tip, Lilybeans. You might as well cook on the stove if you're gonna use propane. You want good flavor, you soften up your cedar chips in water first, then sprinkle them over your hot coals. You won't get better tasting burgers anywhere."

I nod, agreeing with her because I want a hamburger like a dying-of-thirst desert walker wants a drink of water.

The burgers are on, sending smoke up into the air to drive out the dog food smell for a little while. We're sitting in our cheap plastic chaise lounges, the kind that want to come along with you when you stand up, that leave red stripes across your skin. We love them.

It's a month since we moved into the house next to the dog food factory, six weeks since we left Dad.

"What do you think, Lilybeans? Should we grill up that pineapple in the fridge too?"

"Definitely."

I swing my legs out and get up from the chaise. It totters back and forth, threatening to collapse.

Mom jumps up from her own plastic contraption with less drama. She's what you might call graceful—one trait I didn't inherit.

We're in the kitchen and Mom's pulling a cutting board out of an almost bare cupboard. I'm grabbing the pineapple. She sets us up and cuts the pineapple in half. We work side-by-side to get the rough scales off the outside. Smoke is puffing out of the barbecue and the whole kitchen smells like smoldering cedar.

"I always feel a little bad cutting up a pineapple," she says.

"Oh yeah? That's pretty weird."

She bumps me with her hip. "You're weird."

"Maybe, but I'm your kid, so that actually says a lot more about you."

She laughs again—chimes tossed by the wind, tinkling and clear. "Got me there, kiddo."

I look at Mom, really look at her. She's happier than I've seen her in ages. Not the fake happy-for-me happy. Happy because we're free, I think. I reach out and touch her floating curls with my fingertips.

"You'll get me sticky."

"Your hair's like cotton balls."

"White and fluffy? You saying I'm old?"

"Soft and floaty. And, yeah, you're old."

She bumps me again and we go back to cutting up

the pineapple.

I point at the strips of bright yellow fruit. "Why does it bother you, cutting it up?"

She frowns a little. "It's like we're taking its life, its essence. The blade slips in— " She slides the knife, point first, behind a row of scales, runs it down the length and strips them off. "And, just like that, you've sliced off its armor. You've left it defenseless."

She picks up a piece of pineapple and pops it in her mouth. "The inside, the fruit, might be delicious, it might be the best thing you've ever tasted, but you've changed it. You've taken away everything that protects it."

Her eyes have gone sad and far away.

"Is that what Dad did to you?"

She looks at me sideways, gauging me. She nods a little and makes her decision. "Yes. It's also what Grandpa Henry did to Dad, what I let him do to both of us and I'm sorry. It's what I hope you'll never let another person do to you. If you can keep the best of you for you and not compromise what you know to be right and true, you might find it's a little better, a little easier to stay happy."

Easy quiet settles between us until we're finished and throwing away the pineapple scales. I'm glad we have quiet moments now. I'm glad we can barbecue pineapple on our own grill and have friends again if we want. I'm glad we can go for walks in the evenings and hikes on the weekends.

The phone rings and my fingers tighten on the pineapple slice I'm holding, squeezing it until juice plops to the cutting board. Squeezing what's left of its life.

"Tell him we're getting ready to eat and that you'll call him back later. He'll pass out and won't remember."

I nod, forget to wash my hands and head toward the phone. This is the way it was when we left. There was peace and there was life until the phone rang.

I wake up in the chaise just before Margie walks

through the door. I've been in the sun too long and I haven't eaten. I feel sick from no food, from too much summer heat, from the memories.

Margie pulls me over to the couch after she puts her bag away.

"How was today?" she asks, like she does every night.

"Today was fine," I say, like I do every night.

She nods and I see her eyes are extra shiny at the corners where a little mascara's gathered. "I picked up a message from Officer Archie. He called my cell, but I had that all-day meeting."

"Yeah, he called me too."

She looks surprised. "He did?"

"Told me about the letter. Says he'll overnight it."

Margie looks like she can't decide if she's mad or relieved.

"It's okay he called me," I say. "It's a letter from Mom. To me."

"I know. I just wasn't sure you were ready."

I shrug. "Is anyone ever?"

"Good point, kiddo. Far too wise for your tender years, methinks."

"He said they haven't found Hank." I don't mean to speak the words, but they come out anyway.

"I wish they would."

"Me too."

Margie watches me and strokes my cheek with her fingertips. "I love you, Lily. I'm sorry for what Hank did."

I nod against her hand. "It's not your fault." These are the words I can think without thinking the other, speak without speaking the other.

"I think maybe it was." She folds her hands in her lap and looks down at them. "Partly, anyway."

"How could it be your fault?"

She plucks a box off a nearby shelf and runs a finger along its rough edges. The box is shiny silver and has copper streaks that look like rainwater dripping down. I wonder if Margie got inspired for this box by looking through a window on a stormy day. The bottom has green stones for feet, one at each corner. Margie lifts the lid and runs one finger inside the empty space. The box's interior is all smooth copper, no raindrops, like when Margie made it, she decided the inside and the outside had different personalities. One stormy, one calm. Finally, she answers. "Because I left him alone with our father."

"You went to school."

"Yes." Margie's still not looking at me. "I knew how he was, though. God, of course I did. I grew up in that house." She finally looks up—anger and shame and terror, all mixed up in Margie's gold flecks. "Things got very bad for your dad after I left. How much do you know?"

"I know Grandpa Henry was poison. I never met him until after Hank went to work for him."

Margie's flashing eyes drop the anger, the shame. Now there's only terror. "You met him? My father?"

"Hank took me once. He never told Mom."

"Did Grandpa Henry say anything to you?"

I shake my head. "He was sick by then. In bed. He never looked at me. Not once. Like I wasn't there."

"That's for the best, believe me."

"Hank said he could never do anything right."

Margie nods. "After Mom died, it was worse. She loved us at least."

"When did Grandma Josephine die?"

"Just before I left for school. Your mom mentioned Hank told her about Grandpa Henry finding his paintings. My mother had been storing them in the attic for years. My father went crazy, destroyed all the paintings and then told Hank if he wanted to be a woman—" Margie shakes her head. "He equated Hank's wanting to be an artist with being less than a man. Anyway, he punished Hank by making him take over where my mother left off. Fetching his evening twelve-pack, cleaning the house, cooking, shopping. He became my father's maid—slave, really—and if things weren't just so, Hank never heard the end of it." Margie puts the silver and copper box with its green stone feet back on its shelf. "Hank wasn't just an artist, you know? He had an artist's soul—temperamental, sure, but sensitive too. He was crushed by my father's rejection. It took him two more years to get away." Margie shakes her head. "Two years alone with that man would make anyone go crazy."

"But then he met Mom."

Margie smiles. "Yes. She was perfect for him. He was still very angry when they met and, at first, it didn't look like they were going to make it, but she saw something in him. She loved him."

This is enough, I decide. It's getting too close, that night. It's creeping up and the bees are starting to hum and I can't think of Hank this way, of my mom this way. Not when she's a dried up potato bug. Not when she's not here to tell me why. "I forgot to eat today."

Margie stares at me. Push, don't push. "You haven't had anything?"

"No."

She touches my cheek again. "You feel hot. Are you sick?" I shake my head, feeling her soft fingers—not a mom thermometer because Margie's never been a mom, but still nice.

"I was out on the patio too long."

"No food and too much sun. Lily, do we need to have a talk about this?"

"No, it's okay. Tomorrow I'll remember. I can make dinner tonight. Can we eat early?"

"Actually, I thought we'd walk up the road and grab something. You up for getting out?"

I look around the apartment that's getting harder to leave every day. Margie's antsy, like she wants to go. She's probably not used to being at home so much.

"Okay," I say. "Sounds good."

We sit outside at a small café and eat cold turkey sandwiches and pasta salad. We're in those cheap plastic chairs that perch on tiptoes and threaten to fold in on themselves when you try to move closer to the table or scoot back. They remind me of the stripy chaises and Mom. My focus: pasta salad. I eat half my meal, which is more than I've eaten in awhile.

"You've lost more weight," Margie says. Her voice is all worry.

"A few pounds," I agree.

"No more, okay? You're thin enough."

"Okay." I sit carefully back in my wobbly chair, trying to keep it on all four legs.

"I spoke with Dr. Pratchett," Margie says, then waits for me to respond.

"He said you might," I say, hoping these are the

right words. I'm not sure what Margie wants.

"Does it bother you that I might know what you're talking about with Dr. Pratchett?"

"No."

"Because I want you to be able to talk to him openly. But to help you at home, I need to understand more than you're willing to share with me right now. Make sense?"

"Sure. It doesn't bother me."

She nods. "I'm glad." I can see she is, too. "Shall we head back?" She's paid the bill and the waitress has wrapped my sandwich up in an earth-friendly paper box. You won't find Styrofoam in Queen Anne.

"Sure." I get up from the table, holding onto my chair so it doesn't go flying off.

"Let's go a different way and look at some of the big houses. Sound good?"

"Okay."

Margie links her arm through mine and we walk up Queen Anne Hill and look at the mansions. I wonder if any of the people living in them are as happy as me and Mom were in our dog food house. I wonder if the kids slice pineapple for barbecues and string popcorn for Christmas. I wonder if the dads bring guns into the living room and turn people into potato bugs.

My thread's growing too big. I focus on my feet taking one step after another. Right-left-right-left. I think about Margie's arm through mine. I use her as a tether, a touchstone.

Pretty soon I think the bees have changed their sound when I hear a loud *meeeeeewwwww* and then another. We're close to a string of expensive neighborhood boutiques with no one else around. Now I wonder if I'm going crazy. Crazier. "Do you hear that?"

Margie's looking left and right, back to left.

"Where's it coming from?"

I walk faster than I have in awhile, so fast Margie barely keeps up. I follow the *meeewwwws* to a row of dumpsters and lift the lid on the one that's meowing.

"Oh my god," Margie says.

I boost myself up, swing my legs over cowboy-style and land in coffee grounds and banana peels and earth-friendly takeaway boxes. The kitten, not more than six weeks old, is sitting on an overturned coffee can, her mouth open wide, her pink tongue vibrating with the force of her meows. Her black and white fur is gray with dirt. She looks like she's stuck a paw in an electrical socket. I see right away she's a spaz.

I pick her up and her tiny body is all fierce shaking and loud purrs. She goes immediately to my shoulder and sticks her nose in my ear. I laugh. Right out loud, I laugh. It's an odd sound, not like it was before. Not like Mom's. No tinkle, no music. Instead it's muffled, flat.

Margie takes the kitten and hugs her to her chest while I climb out of the dumpster. She looks at me and smiles. "You laughed," she says. "I love your laugh, Lilybeans." I guess she didn't hear the muffled weirdness, or maybe she thought it was the acoustics of the big metal dumpster. My laughing made Margie happy anyway and that counts for something.

I'm out of banana peels and on clean concrete again. I reach for the kitten and bunch up my sweater so she can nestle down in it. She's too interested in my ear, though, and climbs back to my shoulder, sticking her nose in again. I'm getting grimy, but I don't mind. Everything Mom made is washable, practical.

"There's no use making something if you have to leave it on a hanger to enjoy it, Lilybeans. Stuff is meant

to be used. We're not here long enough to let things sit around and collect dust."

"We should take her home, get some food in her," I say.

Margie nods. "We can keep her if you want."

"Okay, I'd like that."

I feel something in me and I don't mind the feeling—a lightness that's more air than tin, not so hollow. Like with Cheetah. I think this kitten will be a good tether. I steady the black and white spaz on my shoulder as we walk down the hill toward Margie's apartment. She's busy purring and nuzzling. Pretty soon she wants to climb down in my arms and when she does, she flops on her back and lets me carry her like a baby.

"She loves you already," Margie says.

"Who throws away a kitten?" I ask. But I know. Mack-Hanks throw away kittens. Mack-Hanks do all kinds of things to cause pain. The lightness in me spreads a little. I think I'm glad because I have a kitten no one else wanted.

Margie shakes her head. "Someone with no idea how precious life is." She strokes the kitten's head with one finger. "Someone with a hole in their chest where their heart should be."

We keep walking.

I name my kitten Binka after a black and white cat on a British cartoon I watched once. My first impression of her was right. She's a spaz. She walks around the apartment on tiptoes and her fur stands straight out from her body, like she's rubbed up against a balloon from head to foot and worked up some static electricity. She's ambitious too, trying to climb Margie's bookcases. I'm guessing when she's older she'll make it to the top. For now she's picked out her favorite three boxes, all on bottom shelves: one too small for her tiny butt, one so big she can stretch out head to tail without touching the ends and a shiny copper one that reminds me of an old-timey bathtub with a lid. This one she bathes on. Of course.

I'm curled up in my favorite chair and the sun's shining on both of us now. It's toasty warm.

Binka's asleep in my lap, stretched out like she's on the Serengeti, a lioness in the shade of some random tree, resting after a big gazelle meal. I stroke her swollen belly and she stretches her little legs out as far as she can. She's kept me here all day—a good tether.

I've finished the Stephen King and moved onto a Cormac McCarthy. It's an end-of-the-world one too. He uses a lot fewer words than King, but I feel the horror of it more, the loss, the desperation. No room for a final stand. No hope. Just what is and what could have been. It's too close to how things are right now, so I set it aside and decide to take a break.

I look around at the books closest to me and pull one off. *Toxic Parents*, the title reads. Pretty soon I'm lost in the stories of adults who were abused as children, but sometimes thought their parents were only strict. I'm halfway finished with chapter three and it occurs to me Grandpa Henry was maybe worse than I thought if Margie had to read these books. Maybe more than poison. I start looking at other titles and realize she's got a pretty big collection on the subject. There's one about emotional blackmail and another about never being good enough, a workbook about life after trauma. I don't touch that one because I think Margie's probably written in it.

I don't remember these books from when Mom and I were here last summer. I think Margie probably put them away when we visited.

A photo album sits on the bottom shelf. The spine has a strange label: "Always Remember." I set Binka on the chair, where she curls up with her nose tucked into her bushy tail, and then pull the album onto my lap. There's a Post-it note inside the cover. The handwriting is Margie's. The note says the same thing as the spine—"always remember." I know I'm snooping now, that I should ask Margie first. But something in me needs to know about the books, about this album, about why Hank was sometimes nice, sometimes mean.

I flip a heavy piece of paper over and stare down at three pictures on the first page—Hank and Margie as kids in the first one. They're still little, Margie maybe seven, Hank five. They're standing in front of Grandpa Henry's house, Hank with a little toy truck, Margie with a ratty teddy bear hugged to her chest, a balloon that says "Happy Birthday" tied around her wrist. She's got a little chocolate or something smeared on her cheek.

Their faces should be smiling, should be happy since it's a birthday, but they're not. What I see in their eyes is what I see in mine now. Hollow.

Grandpa Henry stands away from Grandma Josephine, Margie and Hank. He's staring at the camera, his mouth frowning, his thumbs hooked into the pockets of his workpants. He's wearing a hard hat, like he came home for some lunch and got his picture taken instead.

I don't know what the picture means. I only know Margie and Hank and Grandma Josephine are huddled together while Grandpa Henry stands away from them.

The other two pictures look like they're from the same day, only Hank's crying his eyes out in one and Grandpa Henry's moved closer to them, his hand half-raised. Margie's got one arm around Grandma Josephine's leg, one around Hank's shoulders, her teddy bear dropped in the dust at her feet, her Happy Birthday balloon still floating from her wrist. Her face is turned up to Grandpa Henry now. This one shows more than the hollow, the misery. This one shows her eyes narrowed, her tiny lips pressed together. This expression I know. It's the same one she wore when she told me about leaving Hank behind with Grandpa Henry.

I'm thinking about looking at more pictures when a door opens behind me. I smell whiskey. It's not long before there's mint and paint too. My back's to Margie's living room, one big goose bump. I look over at Binka sleeping in the sunshine and wonder if she smells him too.

"What do you want?"

He doesn't answer.

I slowly put the album back on the shelf and tell the bees to knock it off already. If Hank's here, even if he's a not-Hank, I have to stay around. Binka needs me. I reach for her, touch my fingertips to her spaz fur, smile a little when she stretches and purrs.

With my touchstone, the bees are manageable. Even with the smell I stay. When I finally face him, he's over by the front door. He's wearing the same flannel, same jeans with dark stains, same work boots and there's the same flat light in his eyes. Memories I don't want from that night come back. Memories I don't want from just before we left come along with them. I keep my fingertips on Binka to make myself not disappear.

"Be over in just a minute, sweetheart... I love you, Beans... We'll all be together now... Hold real still, honey... See you soon."

The room twists around me and I'm back at the house where we lived with Hank.

"Where's Mom?"

Dad looks at me from where he's reclined in his barcalounger. "What business is it of yours where your mother is?"

I back out of the room, careful to keep my eyes on my shoes. "Sorry."

I go fast, silent to my room, hoping he stays where he is, hoping he forgets all about me. I should've known better with the half-empty bottle of whiskey shoved between his legs. I hear the squeak and thump of the recliner and heavy, staggering footsteps across the shabby living room, down the shabby hall, outside my chipped and faded bedroom door.

"If this door is locked, you're grounded for a month." His words slip around each other, a slurred mess too heavy for his tongue.

The knob twists. I watch it move from where I'm sitting on my bed. It rotates slowly and then the door swings open. The hinges are squeaky, like the sound they use in horror movies.

"Do you ever do anything on your own?"

I lift the book I'm reading. "I read."

He steps into the room, looking around with one hand on his hip, the other holding the neck of the bottle that lets him be someone else. "Don't be smart with me, Lily. Don't ever talk back to me." He's had too much whiskey to be Dad anymore, past the point of reason, beyond talking normal to. When I look at Dad with his half-empty bottle of whiskey, I think we'll be here forever. The Dad I knew is dead and buried and never coming back. Even if we leave this place, these moments will always be. I can't get out of them.

"Sorry." I open my book again and pretend to read, hoping he'll get bored.

"Look at me when I'm speaking to you."

I keep my head down while I roll my eyes to his. Almost the same, our eyes. His, dark with rage. Mine, dark with hurt. Same color, but so different.

"You rely too much on your mother. You know that?"

I stay focused so it will be over faster.

"You need to be more independent. You understand me? There's no room in this family for spoiled brats." He raises his finger and stabs the air. "Grow up, Lily."

He lifts the bottle and takes a swig, pulling his lips back in a grimace. I wonder for the millionth time why he drinks something that obviously tastes so bad.

For a second, between the whiskey burning his throat and burning his belly, Dad is Dad again. The crinkles at the corners of his eyes smooth out, his lips tremble. I can see him fighting to stay, fighting the war against Grandpa Henry's voice. The person I love, my father, is trying to hold onto himself. But the Hank inside him, his father's son, is too strong. Hatred. Venom fed from the bottles he clutches like life-preservers. I want to tell him he's more than nothing, that there is life, love, hope in him, but the second passes and his eyes are flat again with no light. These moments of seeing my father are almost done.

He turns to go. "God, you're pathetic." His words are soft like his mouth, like his thinning brown hair. The softness is what makes it true. If he screamed it, if he got in my face and yelled, it would be easy to shut out his meaning.

Binka pounces to my shoulder and twitches her tail across my cheek. I ignore the headache coming on and remind myself she's kept me here, kept the bees away. When I don't see the not-Hank anymore, I think maybe she's made him go too. I reach up and scratch her neck. "Binka the magic kitten," I whisper.

She sticks her nose in my ear.

I'm trying to remember where Margie keeps her aspirin when the doorbell rings. Everything inside me bubbles at once because I know who's on the other side of that front door. It doesn't matter if he's Hank or a not-Hank. What matters is the three or four bees buzzing their peace song. I want to go, can't go. I want to fight him, can't fight. I want to find a thread, can't focus. The chain on the door bounces and rattles when he knocks. My smart feet are ready to walk on over. They know a not-Hank wouldn't knock, that he doesn't need a key to get in, that whoever's out there is someone different.

Binka's already trotted over, is sitting in front of the door, peering up at the peephole like she knows that's where you look to see who's knocking. I half expect her to walk right up the door and twist the knob.

The bell ding-dongs again. "Delivery for Lilliana Berkenshire!" someone shouts through the door.

The bubble pops and I feel my whole body breathe. Not Hank. My legs shake underneath me when I stand and walk toward the door.

Binka's got her head twisted around. She's looking at me with her whiskers bunched up. *You're taking too long,* her expression says. *There are new people on the other side of that door to worship me and say I'm pretty. Hurry up, strange human.*

I look through the peephole. It's a Fed Ex delivery guy. I've been waiting and not waiting for Mom's letter, trying not to think about it.

I open the door.

"Good afternoon," he says. "I was beginning to think no one was home." He gives me a big smile when Binka scales me and sits on my shoulder.

"Sorry," I say.

"Oh, no worries." He nods at Binka. "Cute kitten."

"Thanks." I'm looking at the flat orange and white cardboard in the guy's hand. I'm watching it like it's going to disappear if I don't keep total focus.

"Are you Lilliana Berkenshire?" he asks after he takes a peek at his electronic clipboard.

I nod because I can't take my eyes off the bright parcel, can't get a word out. Mom's last letter is in there. Mom's letter to me.

I'm reaching for the clipboard and signing my name. The letters don't look like letters, but he seems satisfied, pushes a few buttons and turns to go.

"Have a nice day," he says.

I grunt something, close the door, lock up, latch the chain.

I reach up to steady Binka as we head back to

our sun chair. She hops off my shoulder when I sit down, then runs sideways with her tail arched and electrified. She disappears into our bedroom while I sit by myself and commence staring at the thin cardboard in my hands. I stare so hard at the part that says "pull here," complete with arrows just in case you don't know which way to go with the pulling, that my eyes start to burn a little. I flip the cardboard over and stare at my name in Officer Archie's all-caps handwriting. Binka scratching in her litter box and meowing quietly to herself wakes me up a little. I need to blink and when I do there are tears.

I "pull here" and the package opens. I'm left with a curled strip of cardboard I set aside for Binka. She'll go full spaz when she sees it, probably hide it behind a bookcase like she does her kibble.

There are two envelopes inside. One says "For Lily, from Archie." The other simply says "Lilybeans." The one with Lilybeans is in my mom's calligraphic handwriting.

I stare at the letters for a long time. The bees start up with their humming—a full hive, no messing around with just one or two. Before I go I notice a pattern in the buzzing. There are the bees and then quiet and then the bees again. The pattern repeats once before I'm pulled in.

When I come back, I've still got the letters in my hands and my cell phone's playing a tune. Binka's curled up in my lap again, asleep. A whole hour's gone by according to the clock on the wall.

I shake my head and reach for the phone on the table next to me. Binka's cardboard strip is gone. I missed her full spaz.

"Hello?"

"Lily? Where have you been?" Margie is panicked.

"Hi. Sorry, I didn't hear the phone. I was napping." The lie is easy when I think about Margie's fear.

She's quiet for a minute. "Really napping or the other?"

"Napping. Honest, Aunt Margie. Mom's letter came." I know this will distract her.

"Have you read it?"

"No, not yet. Should I wait until you come home?"

"What do you think? It's up to you. I could read it with you or we could take it to Dr. Pratchett's."

"Okay. I'll think about it."

"I love you."

"Okay."

Before I put the phone away, I snap a few pictures of Binka's sleeping face and make her my phone's wallpaper so I can see her whenever I want. My always-tether, Binka. *Click. Snap.*

I open Officer Archie's letter first. Between the tear-prisms and the scratchy handwriting, I can barely read the note. Luckily it's just a single sentence.

Lily,

I hope this letter finds you well. Please call if you have any questions at all.

A Utah number is scribbled under his name at the bottom. I set the note on the table next to me. Like it's inspired her to get clean, Binka stretches on her tiptoes, hops on the table, sits on Officer Archie's phone number and starts bathing her face.

I hold Mom's letter for a long time, then flip it over. It's not sealed, but it's been carefully opened, not ragged like I expect. I slip a couple fingers inside and pull the letter out. It's not your typical notebook paper. Not for Mom. She loved stationary and she used her fanciest for my letter. It's one page long. Four short paragraphs. The date is two days before Hank came. There's a "Love, Mom" at the bottom, a "Dear Lily" at the top and a lifetime of words in between.

Dear Lily,

If you're reading this, it is for one of two reasons: either you've gone snooping, which you rarely do, or something happened and I've had to leave you. No matter how old you are, it's too soon. I'm sorry and I love you.

My sweet Lilybeans, it's important you listen to me now. Read this letter out loud and listen to my words. Pretend I'm with you. Hear my voice. It's that important. Are you reading out loud? Good girl.

Your father said things to you that were not true. He said things about me and about you, and he lied. I have regrets, Lilybeans. I let us stay too long and I let him harass you after we left. He said things to make me believe we could go back to the way we once were. I was naïve, too hopeful. I'm sorry. I'm not brave like you are, my darling.

I pause for a minute and let Mom's words sink in. She thought I was brave. I thought she was. We each believed we were the weak one.

You are brilliant. You are beautiful. You are the best person I've ever known. Your heart is bigger than the world. I look into your eyes and I see the woman you will become. Your gentle ways, your spirit, your ability to see the good in others, these things will attract people to you when you're older, sweet girl. I know friends are scarce right now, but it's a matter of time before someone glimpses that soul of yours and when they do, they'll never let you go. I wish so much I could hold a mirror up and show you what I see. All I can do is hope you will read this and believe me. I never lied to you. Not once. Your father had it wrong and I will always feel pity that he chose the path he did and pushed us away. And I will always feel lucky that we had our time together, that you are my daughter, my girl, my Lilybeans. I'll be waiting for you up ahead. Take your time and have a beautiful life. And remember, life is beautiful. I took so many pictures of you because I wanted to remember that. With all my heart, I love you.

Love,
Mom

I hold the letter for a long time and feel myself rip inside. It's a tiny hole, a puncture. Inside the rip is peace and quiet. I feel it there, waiting. I can go, it says. I can stay if I want to. I don't have to keep stuffing. I can just let go and be gone.

I look over at Binka washing her whiskers. I want to hold onto my kitten, to the beauty I see in her. I think I understand how I helped Mom—I was her always-tether. I think about Binka's whiskers. Only her whiskers. They keep me here.

I let the tears drop one by one onto Mom's beautiful handwriting. The letters smear a little. My tears, her ink, together. No matter what happens with Hank's promise to come for me, a part of Mom and a part of me will be here. Always. I fold the stationary back up, put it in its envelope and hold it against my chest.

Binka stops bathing and stares at me with huge green eyes. All her fur is straight out from her body and the ends are shining in the filtered sunlight streaming through the window next to us. She tips her head to the side. Her ears are huge and all the way forward. She's trying to figure me out. Being the spaz she is, she lets out a trill twice her size and launches. She lands on my shoulder, smashes her forehead to my cheek and starts purring in big, looping reverberations. I can feel her whole body, nose to tail, vibrating with the power of those purrs.

"You're crazy, you know that?"

She trills again and rubs my head with everything she's got, leaving her tail to twitch up my nose. This makes me laugh so hard the rip widens. Laughing and crying are right there together, so I quiet down quickly, go back into that small space where I don't lose time, but I can still be. I stay here for Binka and for Margie.

My thread: Binka's whiskers.

I show Margie the letter and she cries. She cries for a good ten minutes, but they're not all grief tears.

"Did you read it out loud, like she said?" Margie's asks in a watery voice.

"No, maybe another time."

"Your mom was a special woman, Lily. She loved you more than anything." She stares at me for a minute and I watch the tears in her eyes amplify the gold flecks. "Did you know that?"

"I always knew," I say, but it's too much, talking about Mom's letter. I turn to the bookcase nearest me and pull out a random book. "Why do you have these?"

Margie's still for another minute, making up her mind to let me stay quiet or push. Finally she looks down at the book's title and swivels her head to see it better. It's the one about never being good enough.

"You have a lot of these," I say, pointing up, down, right, left.

"Yes. Some have helped me cope."

"I don't want to pry."

"You can ask me anything."

"Grandpa Henry was more than just mean?"

Margie nods. "He was verbally, emotionally and sometimes physically abusive."

I feel my eyes narrow and the buzzing starts up. Baby bees in my ears. I tell them to wait, please wait.

"He was a cruel man, Lily. He…" She glances around the room. "He never knew when to stop."

"What about Grandma? Didn't she protect you?"

"No. She was in the same boat. I was mad at her for a long time because she didn't take us and leave, but I guess part of me understood why." Margie smiles sadly. "My father never would have allowed it anyway. He would've found us and dragged us back to that old house kicking and screaming, all the while complaining about the miles he had to put on his truck to find us."

"I guess he hurt Hank too. I mean more than just yelling, more than telling him not to do art."

Margie nods. "Did you know Hank couldn't swing a hammer to save his life?"

"Yeah. I believe it." We were always having to call repair guys to our house because Hank didn't know you could just restart a pilot light or press the reset button on a garbage disposal. Hank liked to say that his hands were made to hold paint brushes, not tools.

I don't want these memories. It's his being a normal dad once that's the worst.

"Our father, well, he hurt Hank with a hammer

once."

I look up quickly into Margie's sad eyes. "His crooked finger?"

She nods.

"Grandpa Henry smashed Hank's finger because he couldn't hammer a nail?"

"He did."

I think on this awhile. Hank always said he smashed his own finger, called himself a klutz, blamed the crookedness for not being able to paint the way he wanted. "Do you think maybe if Hank hadn't gone to work for Grandpa Henry…?"

Margie's eyes widen a little. "Oh, honey, I don't know. Your mom said things were bad sometimes, that Hank was drinking more and more, even before my father called."

"Yeah," I say quietly. "After he stopped painting."

"He stopped believing he had talent."

"I guess. Aunt Margie?"

She takes my hand and squeezes it tight. "Yes, kiddo?"

I look left, right, up, down at all the boxes Margie's made. Silver and copper and gold, some dull, some shiny, some square, some rectangle, some round. Not a single box looks the same as another. One is so dark it looks like leather, a pretty crane with some yellow flowers on its lid. One is so light it looks like creamy milk, even shaped like one of those old fashioned milk bottles, only a lot shorter and with a ridged lid. "You have a lot of these metal boxes. I mean, they're cool, but did you ever think about making something else? You know, like a lamp or some coasters or a sword? Is it like creative constipation or something?"

Margie's head cocks. "Well lookie there. That's the Lilybeans I remember." She jumps up from the couch, grabs the biggest box off the top of the bookcase—the one you could store an old-timey dictionary in. It's a copper one, looks like it's made out of this delicate shale my geology teacher showed us once. All flaking, layered metal and uneven surfaces. Margie plucks it off like it weighs nothing. When she hands it to me I expect it to sink to my lap, too heavy to hold since it's so big. Instead it's lighter than Binka. I run my fingers along its rough lid, surprised it doesn't flake off on my fingertips like the shale did in class. I flip it over. Margie's initials are etched into one corner. The box's lid doesn't come off, just a decorative piece to give it symmetry or whatever.

"It's so light," I say.

Margie grins and walks to the other side of the room. She scoots a tiny box off a shelf into her cupped hand and comes back to the couch. I put the big box aside and take the small one. It's heavy, as heavy as I expected the big one to be. I let it sink to my lap, holding it in one hand on my thigh. This one's silver all the way around, smooth with rounded corners. Instead of a lid it has a leaf on top—a leaf with little raindrops sitting like bubbles on the surface.

"I thought this one would be light. How did you find metal like this?"

"I didn't find the metal at all. I made it. My own recipe. Behold, the power of metallurgy!" Margie's grinning big and her eyes are shiny with excitement. She plucks another small box off a nearby shelf. This one's copper with a nice patina, a working lid that opens to a black velvety inside. She hands it to me. Light as a feather again. "It's not the size or the shape that determines its weight." She points to the giant shale box sitting next to me on the couch. "I'll bet you think that one's pretty strong because it's big, huh?"

I nod.

"Of every box here, it's the most fragile. One good drop and it would shatter into a million pieces." She smiles a little. "You wouldn't know it by looking at it, right?"

I'm turning the little silver box over and over in my hands, running my fingers across its bubbled raindrops, its weight comforting.

"That one you're holding, though, is one of the toughest in the bunch." Margie plucks Binka off the floor where she's been washing her face. The kitten looks indignant for about a second before she's on Margie's shoulder, shoving her face in Margie's pixie cut. "Kinda like this little bugger. Tiny on the outside, tough on the inside. I guess that's why I love my job so much. I get to make surprises."

I keep my eyes on the box and my voice down. "Hank showed me the tin cry once."

"He did?"

"Yes."

Margie reaches out and touches my hand where it's smoothing the silky metal. "It's a little freaky, huh?"

"Yeah." To me it sounded like an animal dying. Six years old and Hank bending a piece of tin, making me listen real close. I didn't like it and ran away when I heard the screams from the twisting metal.

"Lily?" Dad's outside my bedroom door, knocking softly. "You okay, kiddo?"

I'm sitting on my bed, hugging my floppy-eared stuffed Pluto to my chest. Dad opens the door slowly and sticks his head in.

I'm mad and don't mind letting him see it. He's hurt and doesn't mind letting me see it. Same eyes, different emotions.

"I thought you'd like that, Lilybeans." His voice is low, like when he's talking to Mom about his boss embarrassing him in front of everybody at work.

When I don't say anything, he smiles sadly, backs away and closes the door softly behind him.

"Did the tin break?" Margie's asking.

"I ran away before it could."

"It doesn't always, you know."

"Break?"

"Right. Sometimes it just ends up in a different shape. The tin cries, sometimes even screams and then becomes something else, often something beautiful." Margie reaches behind her, grabs another box and hands it to me. This one is dull silver, all one piece, no lid, light as a feather. "Like this little guy. He's made from a single sheet, gently bent until he became the shape I wanted."

"Did it cry?"

"Oh yeah," Margie says. "But look how beautiful it is now. Tin isn't very interesting just flat. It's got a lot more character when it's been stressed and molded. The only way to do that is to bend it until it cries."

The tin box seems even more delicate than the rough and fragile one on the couch next to me. It feels like one more bend and it could break. I hand it back to Margie, keeping an eye on her hands to make sure she's not going to make it cry again. She puts it back on its shelf.

"Grandpa Henry bent Hank too much," I say to my hands. "Broke him."

Nothing but silence.

Finally, I look up and Margie's staring at me with big eyes. "All this time and I'd never thought of it like that." She brushes my arm, keeping me here even with the bees coming on stronger. "I think it's a little dangerous to blame it all on Grandpa Henry, though."

"Because you turned out okay."

"That's the thing you can't predict. Some people, they respond to life so differently than others would in the same situation." She watches me for a minute, then makes a decision. "Hank used to get in fights when we were kids. Did you know that?"

"No, I didn't know."

"I guess it was his way of dealing with my father's abuse. He put one kid in the hospital when we were in high school. After our mother died, I suspect it got much worse."

I watch Aunt Margie for awhile and think about Grandpa Henry and Hank, about choices and bendy tin.

"Mom knew Grandpa Henry hurt you and Hank," I say. "Mom knew Hank hurt other people." It's why he had a different uniform shirt every year. Hank couldn't get along with his coworkers, kept getting in fights, quitting his jobs or getting fired.

"Yes." Margie anticipates my next question and answers it before I ask. "But she never would have guessed this could happen."

"Hank hit her once."

Margie nods. "I know and your mom said he was very sorry afterward."

"He split her cheek right open. She had to have stitches."

Margie's lips are moving, but the buzzing is full force now. It fills my head and my ears, wants to ask its own questions. It wants to ask how Mom could fall in love with Hank, marry him, have a baby. It wants to ask how things got this far, how she ended up a potato bug on our living room floor, how Hank ended up a broken tin man, how I ended up a hollow tin girl.

❧

"Lily?"

"I'm back, Aunt Margie. I'm sorry."

Margie's holding both my hands now and Binka's sitting on my shoulder. She smashes her forehead into my neck when I come to.

"Lily, don't apologize. It's not your fault."

"How long this time?"

"Longer."

I move the curtains aside. It's dark out. "Hours."

"Just one. I called Dr. Pratchett. He said to wait a little longer."

Margie's eyes are full of fear again. I look away.

"Has anything changed about your quiet place? Is it still nothing?"

I nod and pluck Binka off my shoulder, give her a kiss and put her on my lap. "Yes. Still nothing. Peaceful. I'm sorry."

"No, don't apologize. Dr. Pratchett will help you. You'll get better."

I pet Binka where she's roar-purring in my lap.

Margie waits a little longer—a pause to let me know she's not finished, that she has something to say. "It's been almost a month, kiddo. I'm not supposed to pester you, but I want you to know I'm here. If you ever want to talk, I'm here."

Binka stretches when I stroke her belly.

"Lilybeans?"

I look up at my aunt who's trying so hard. I want to ask her about Hank, if she's scared, if she's seen him too. What's in her eyes is too much already, though. Grandpa Henry, my spells, Hank, fear—all reflected in Margie's blue and gold.

"Did you hear me?"

Nod.

"I see the pain in you," she says. "I see what it's

costing to keep it all inside. I remember when I started treatment with Dr. Pratchett. It was the same for me. There was so much grief, so much anger, so many questions. I didn't know where to begin because I was afraid I wouldn't know how to stop."

I'm looking down at Binka, focusing on one black spot. "One black spot," I say.

"What's that?" Margie asks.

"Did you ever notice how Binka has this one black spot that's not like the others?" I touch it with my fingertip and the kitten stretches so hard her tiny claws pop out, smaller than blades of new grass.

Margie leans in and rubs the fur down. "You're right. Star-shaped."

"Yeah."

She pats my hand. "She's our little star."

"Spastic star."

I trace the outline of Binka's star spot and think about how it's not like any of her other spots, how it's a hidden surprise. Like Margie's boxes—some light, some heavy, some big, some small, but all of them not like they seem. Margie's a metallurgist because she likes to be surprised, because she doesn't know how something's going to turn out until she gives it a try.

I think I used to be like that. I think I used to write poems and stories because I liked being surprised. Now the surprises send me to the quiet place where I don't have to think or be. With my fingertips on Binka, with her hidden star right there for me to see, I wonder if maybe someday I'll get to feel surprised again without the bees carrying me off.

It's Thursday again and I'm on the bus, chugging along toward Dr. Pratchett's office. Margie's having a crisis at work—people yelling in the background when she called. She sounded mad and asked if I could make it okay on the bus. I told her I'd be fine.

I'm tapping my knee, ready to be heading back to the apartment already. I wonder if Dr. Pratchett will let me go early. My focus: get Dr. Pratchett to let me go early.

I climb down from the bus when it stops at the big glass building and walk past the dancing fountains, noticing for the first time there are lights under the water. I wonder what it looks like at night. Colors shooting up, up, up, crashing back down into flat stillness, I think. I'm through the two sets of glass doors and the guard at the front desk is smiling at me. I nod politely, then watch my feet, put one right in front of the other until I'm riding the elevator up.

I'm waiting in the waiting room, focusing on my thread—get Dr. Pratchett to let me go early—so I don't hear when he opens the door.

"Hello, Lily." He's casual today, jeans and a light blue oxford shirt. Tennies on his feet. I doubt he's got argyle socks stuffed inside the ragged canvas.

"Hi, Dr. Pratchett."

"Would you like to come in?"

I walk past him holding the door open for me and go right to the chair I sat in last week. "I'm hoping to leave early," I say.

"Oh? Why is that?"

"I have a new kitten at home. She hasn't been without me since I found her."

Dr. Pratchett smiles, looking pleased. "Well, that's perfectly understandable. It's important we keep our full time, though. I hope you understand."

I shrug and pluck at my sweater. I'm still wearing the one Mom knitted, washed a few times since I found Binka. It's getting hot and I think I'll have to stop wearing it so much. The chocolate is starting to turn beige and I wonder if pretty soon I'll have to put it on a hanger to preserve it.

"Wear it 'til it falls apart, Lilybeans."

Deep breath.

Dr. Pratchett's sitting in the chair opposite me now and his white fluffy eyebrows are raised. "What's your kitten's name?"

"Binka," I say.

"Is she black and white?"

I feel my eyes widen a little. "You've see that show?"

"British, right?"

"Yeah."

"Where did you find her?"

"In a dumpster."

He pauses and looks confused. "You mean *near* a dumpster?"

"No, I mean in."

"I don't understand, Lily. Someone put the kitten in a dumpster?"

"Yeah, I guess someone did."

"What do you think about that?"

I look toward the nearest bookshelf and pick out a title. *Moby Dick* is my new thread. I repeat *Call me Ishmael* and *There is a wisdom that is woe; but there is a woe that is madness*. I think of whales and blow holes, of gliding alone through silky, clear water. I don't think about whaling boats or spears.

"People throw things away all the time," I say because it's true.

"But Binka isn't a thing."

I look Dr. Pratchett in the eyes. "She was to someone."

"Do you mean if someone had seen her as more than just a thing they wouldn't have thrown her away?"

Call me Ishmael. "No, I mean some people see everybody as a thing, everybody as something to be thrown away. Margie said when we found her that 'some people don't know how precious life is.' I think it's more like some people don't care." *Moby Dick.*

Dr. Pratchett has this amazed look on his face, but his eyes are sad. I focus on his big sailing trophy.

"You're a very wise young woman," he says.

I don't scoff, but I want to. Instead, I start reading book spines. "You have a lot of fiction here."

"I love fiction."

"Yeah, me too," I say, my voice soft, distracted while I scan the titles. I get up when I see a familiar design. "You own *The Stand*?" I ask and run my fingers down the hardback spine, tracing each of the engraved letters.

"Yes, in fact, that's a first edition. Signed by The King himself."

I glance over my shoulder. "You met him?"

"He came to Seattle for a book signing when it was first published. I stood in line for more than an hour and shook the man's hand myself." Dr. Pratchett looks proud he waited a whole hour to meet the king of horror.

I admit, I'm impressed and I like this thread better than *Moby Dick*. "What was he like?"

"Normal." Dr. Pratchett's pride deflates and he sounds disappointed, like he's been holding a grudge for more than twenty years.

"You expected something else?"

He perches on the edge of his chair. "I guess I did."

"What? 666 carved into his forehead? Bats under his hat? A crow for a pet?"

Dr. Pratchett's laughing now. "Something like that."

I turn back to the bookshelf, shaking my head. I'm still caressing the letters on the binding. "It's my favorite book. I've read it three times."

"Why is it your favorite?"

"I don't know."

"Is it the idea of starting over?"

I think about this for a minute, remembering my words when Mom asked why I liked the book so much. I let the memory go quickly. "Maybe," I say to placate him.

"Lily?"

I walk back to my chair and sit down.

"Let's keep on with this thread, okay?"

Thread. *King book signing.* I see his dark, tousled hair, his unhandsome face, his eyes that have known success and failure and pain. *King.*

Dr. Pratchett pushes. "Why do you think *The Stand* is your favorite book? Of all the books you've read, why it?"

I'm watching my feet tap once, twice, three times. I look back up at Dr. Pratchett. He's waiting for me to say something. "I like Stu Redman. He's a good character."

Dr. Pratchett smiles. "He was my favorite in the book. He's a strong man, a stand-up guy, as King would say. Why do you like him in particular?"

I think about how Stu and Frannie get together, how Stu takes care of her even though she's pregnant with another guy's kid. "It's that stand-up thing, like you said. It's that he gets how important every life is, including Frannie's baby. You know? Even though it's not his?"

"That makes a lot of sense."

"I wanted Hank to be more like Stu," I say to my hands. "Stu wouldn't have spent his nights drinking six packs."

"May I ask you a question about your father?"

"Okay."

"How do you feel about him now?"

I suck in my breath and try not to have another coughing fit. A wildfire starts in my belly and wants to burn right through to my heart. I try to breathe flames to let it go, to blow out the black smoke filling up my lungs. I'm all charcoal and ash in there though, burned up and empty.

The phone rings. I pick it up on the third shrill buzz.

"Whatcha up to, Beans?"

"Just studying."

"What's your mother doing?" His words slur so "mother" comes out "mutter."

"I'm not sure."

"Beans, you know she sleeps with every guy she meets, don't you? You know you're poor for no reason?"

"Okay, Dad."

"Don't treat me like I'm a child."

"I'm not."

"You don't believe me."

I stay silent. This is the part where I never know how to answer.

"She hides money, Beans. You wouldn't believe how much."

"Why would she do that?" I try to keep the frustration out of my voice, try to sound curious instead of skeptical.

"She doesn't want you to have anything nice. She never did."

"Okay, Dad."

"Didn't you always wonder how she could afford expensive clothes? All that jewelry?"

I think about Mom's treasure chest of riches—an engagement ring with a diamond the size of a grain of rice, a matching wedding band, a delicate gold chain with a broken clasp. She never buys a new anything when she can find the same thing secondhand. Even if she wants a blue blouse, she'll settle for pink if it's cheap enough.

He's waiting.

"Sorry, Dad, I didn't know she had a lot of jewelry."

"Are you blind?"

"I don't think so."

"Don't be smart with me, Beans."

"I have a lot of homework, Dad."

He pauses. He's either going to let me go or start pretend-crying. Fake sorries to make me stay.

"Fine, Lily. That's just fine. You go ahead and ignore your old pop who doesn't know what's happening with you anymore. You go ahead and pretend you don't have a father and I'll just talk to you later."

Guilt, the always popular third option.

"Sorry, Dad, I just have a big test tomorrow."

He slams the phone down hard so it sends a big bang down my ear canal. Then a dial tone—my best friend.

Dr. Pratchett sits forward and touches my hand. "I know this is difficult, but I think it's important we keep going. Is that okay with you?"

I shrug and imagine my *King book signing* thread stretching out in front of me. I imagine Dr. Pratchett snagging the thread here and there, making new little paths I can go down or not go down. I tell myself I don't have to follow those snags with my whole mind, that I can stay on *King* and still help Dr. Pratchett understand.

"What's the first word that comes to mind when you think of your father?"

"Hank," I say.

Dr. Pratchett looks confused.

I let him off the hook. "It's his first name. I can't think of him as my father anymore."

Dr. Pratchett's nodding now, like this is the best news he's heard all day. "Okay, good, Lily. Why do you think that is?"

"What does it matter?"

"I think it matters quite a bit. For example, I suspect the episodes you experience have a lot to do with how you feel about your father, and especially about what he did."

I think on Dr. Pratchett's words. "There's a buzzing before each spell," I say.

"What kind of buzzing?"

I take a deep breath and sink down into the leather, letting it smoosh up around me. "Like bees, but also there's a pattern."

Dr. Pratchett's nodding. I expect to see he thinks I'm crazy, but he's excited. "And what do you think the pattern is?"

I cross my arms and shake my head. "I don't know."

"I'd like you to think about the buzzing you hear. You said it sounds like bees?" His voice is soothing, like he's trying out some hypnosis on me.

"Yes."

"Now think about the pattern."

"Okay."

"What does the pattern remind you of?"

"There's the buzzing and then there's silence and then the buzzing again." I feel my eyes go wide. "It's a phone ringing. The phone in my old house."

Dr. Pratchett's nodding. "Is the phone in your old house important?"

"You're poor for no reason, Lily."

"It used to ring a lot. I think it's an old memory."

I look at the clock on Dr. Pratchett's desk. "It's almost time to go."

He doesn't look at the clock, but stays focused on me. "Just about." He watches me and I see he wants to press. It's the same look Margie gets. We're all walking narrow paths. Push, don't push.

Today it's push.

"Can you tell me why the phone in your old house is significant?"

I don't think I can say the words.

"In here you're completely safe. You can say anything."

"It was my fault." My words come out like fire. They spray the room, me, Dr. Pratchett, burning us both to ash. My voice is deep, filtered by the rip that wants to open wide.

"What was your fault?"

"That night. It was my fault. Hank called first. If I'd picked up the phone, if I'd talked to him until he was done lying about her, she'd still be alive." I say this in a rush, like it's been sitting down inside me, a big wad of awful swallowing me whole. I can't stop thinking about Mom's letter, about how she wrote it two days before Hank came with his gun, how I could've found the letter forty years from now if I'd only answered the phone.

I breathe.

"Stay with me, Lily," Dr. Pratchett says. "Tell me about these phone calls. Did your dad call often?"

"Hank. Almost every night."

"What did he say?"

"Did you know she's hiding money? Did you know you're poor for nothing? Did you know she's sleeping with every guy she meets? Did you know your mother's a slut and a whore? Did you know, Lily, did you?"

"Terrible things about my mother. Untrue things." Things that made me question my thrift store clothes, question Mom when she got home from work an hour late, made me hate my father for making me doubt her.

"When did your parents separate?" Dr. Pratchett's asking.

"We left a year ago."

"And he called you often?"

"When he was drunk. We didn't talk if he wasn't."

"Did your mother ever ask Hank to stop calling?"

"She tried once. He came over instead. It was bad. After that I told Mom I would handle it. She would sometimes tell me not to answer, but I always did anyway. Except..."

"That last night?"

"If I'd just stuck to the rules. His rules."

"Lily, if you hear nothing else from me, I'd like you to hear this. Are you listening?"

"Yes."

"What happened is not your fault. We cannot control the choices other people make. As hard as it is to accept, I don't think it would have mattered if you'd answered or not." He says each word like they weigh three tons each.

I watch Dr. Pratchett awhile. If I was Binka, my ears would be all the way forward. "Why?"

"When Margie and I talked after your first visit, she told me Hank went to work for his father what? A year or so before you left?"

Nod.

"She also said Hank did this because he believed his father would leave him an inheritance, quite possibly the family metal works business?"

"Yeah. Even though Da—Hank—didn't want to install rain gutters."

"But your grandfather didn't name him in the will."

"No."

"Lily, from what Margie's told me about your mother, Hank contacted her quite often, usually during work hours. Did you know that?"

I can't find words in me to say anything. Hank called Mom? When? Why didn't she tell me?

"Would you like to hear what they discussed?"

"You know?" My voice is a whisper in this spicy-like-Christmas office. I think there's paint, maybe some whiskey now too, but I ignore these signs of not-Hank, keeping focused on Dr. Pratchett.

"Margie told me. She thought you might feel more comfortable talking about it here."

I focus on my hands and pick at a hangnail. When I look up again, Hank is standing behind Dr. Pratchett's chair. His arms are hanging at his sides and one hand is holding a bottle of whiskey. His smell is too much. I look down at my hands again, wonder if Dr. Pratchett sees me seeing Hank.

"What did he want?" I say.

"I wanted you and your mother to come home," not-

Hank whispers.

I don't look, but I think probably he hasn't moved his lips.

"Well, he missed you both very much," Dr. Pratchett says. Careful like, he says Hank missed us. "He was hoping you might rejoin him again someday."

"But you never did," not-Hank says. "I needed you and you left me."

Dr. Pratchett leans forward again. "Are you okay?"

Am I? No, I am not. There are not-Hanks to think about and kitchen bullets and real-Hank coming for me. There are Margie's metal boxes that mean some things that look weak are strong and some things that look strong are weak. There are the bees, one knocking around right now, buzzing in my ear. And now Hank harassing Mom and I never knew.

Like Dr. Pratchett hears the bees too, he reaches across empty air and touches my hand, keeping me here. "We can discuss this another time if you prefer, Lily."

I glance at the clock. It's after time. "Maybe that's a good idea." I can't hear what Hank said to Mom right now. Can't hear it, can't handle it.

"Just one thing before we end our session. When the phone would start ringing in your house, how would you make it stop?"

I don't look up because I still smell whiskey. "I answered it."

He waits.

"You think I should answer the buzzing?" I say to my hands.

"Did the phone stop ringing when you answered it?"

"Yes." I look at not-Hank behind Dr. Pratchett's chair. His whiskey bottle is gone. He stares at me with dead mantis eyes, then slowly holds up his hands, takes a mock picture of me. *See you later.* For the first time, I see him disappear. *Click. Snap.* Gone.

"What do you think will happen if you answer the buzzing?" Dr. Pratchett asks.

"I'll disappear forever into the quiet place, end up a crazy homeless person talking to invisible people on a street corner. Or die."

"You won't die, Lily, and I don't think you're in danger of losing your mind." Dr. Pratchett smiles. If he knew about the not-Hanks, he'd think something different for sure. "We're here for you, your Aunt and I. I think answering the buzzing may be the next big step in your recovery. Okay?"

"Okay."

"Just one more thing before you go."

"You said that last time."

Dr. Pratchett smiles and gets up from his chair. "The joy of getting old, my dear." He opens a drawer. "I have a workbook I'd like you to begin using as a companion to our sessions."

"Homework?"

"Afraid so."

"Summer school," I mutter under my breath.

He laughs and holds it up for me to see.

"Margie has that one." It's the same workbook I saw on her shelf, the one I didn't look at because I thought she might've written in it.

"It's a good one," he says without acknowledging Margie's been a crazy here even though she told me.

Dr. Pratchett says to work through the book slowly, to not skip or look ahead. I can put it aside if it's too much. I regard it with suspicion.

"It won't bite, Lily, and I believe it will help you. I want you to pay close attention to what the book says about self-care. Sound good?"

"I didn't bring a bag today."

Dr. Pratchett looks confused.

"Sorry, I mean I'd rather not carry that around if it's not in a bag. People are nosy enough without a book that tells them all about my problems."

"Of course," he says and grabs a canvas bag out of a drawer. "I've got plenty of these. You keep it. Carry the book back and forth in it. Okay?"

"Thanks." I take the bag and read the stamped logo. "Twice Sold Tales. Margie and I went here once. It's where Ha—" I look up fast. "It's where this really cute cat decided to use me as a bed."

Dr. Pratchett's eyes go squinty. "Were you going to say something else?"

I shake my head and look down at the workbook in my hands. "I'll start on it tomorrow. Okay?"

I don't look at Dr. Pratchett again, but I feel him watching me. Push, don't push. Right now it's don't push. I've made him late for his next appointment.

"Okay, Lily, sounds good." He walks me over to the secret door. "See you next week?"

I think about Hank at the bookstore, in Margie's apartment and almost say, "I hope so." I manage to keep my mouth shut tight, though, and nod instead.

I trot fast to the elevator, then hit the down button over and over when I get there. I don't watch my reflection or think about my almost telling Dr. Pratchett about the not-Hanks. I think only about Binka home alone and how if I don't get downstairs fast, I'm going to miss my bus.

Finally the elevator doors sweep open with all their dramatic flourish. Empty. I ride down by myself and hit the lobby running. I stop only when I notice bright blond hair and a shiny turquoise blouse out of the corner of my eye. I stop, almost skidding into the guard's desk. He smiles at me and then turns back to the blonde. Tiffany.

"Miss, I'm afraid I can't help you."

Tiffany turns to an older version of herself with the same platinum blond hair, same expensive-type clothes. The woman who's probably Tiffany's mom smiles and tips her head. I don't like her smile. There's nothing soft or kind about her. She's all hard edges and prickly barbs. "Now listen to me, Branson. I will not have you speak to my daughter this way."

Tiffany gets this satisfied look on her face, her eyes glittery in the bright lobby. She watches the guard's face closely.

Tiffany's mom leans forward, unfurls a long, tapered finger with a long, tapered fingernail. "You find that necklace, Branson. If you don't, I'll be forced to believe some not-so-nice things about you, young man." She pretends she's joking.

"Ma'am—"

"What have I told you about that word?"

Poor Branson has moved into dangerous territory. Tiffany's mom's head is lowered like a bull and she's watching him through her eyelashes. She's about a second away from either launching herself across the high countertop to strangle the guard or ask in her fake calm voice to talk with his boss. It's hard to tell which.

"So sorry, Mrs. Spangler," Branson says. It's obvious the security guard's an old hand at this. I imagine Tiffany and her mom give him lots of crap all the time. He's younger than the other guards and has a tattoo on his neck. I'm guessing getting a tattoo on your neck sets you up for a pretty high pain tolerance. Two unhappy, spoiled ladies probably just barely make his radar.

Tiffany's smile is getting bigger and bigger and she's watching Branson with a shiny glint in her eyes, like she's hungry to see him get in trouble.

"Now, my daughter says she left the necklace on this counter. It's a ten-thousand dollar item, Branson." She looks him up down, up again. "I'm sure you can appreciate its value."

"Of course, ma—Mrs. Spangler."

"I'd like you to tell me where it is."

"I'm sorry, but I don't know."

"My daughter says you were the one working when she left it here."

"It's quite possible." Branson keeps his gaze steady, his focus on Mrs. Spangler.

"You realize this could mean your job?"

"I didn't take your daughter's necklace."

"Are you sure about that?"

"Quite sure."

"What, pray tell, do you believe happened to it?" Mrs. Spangler's gone full sarcastic.

"I imagine your daughter forgot where she put it. Perhaps it's in your apartment. Or tucked away in a purse for safe-keeping. Like the ring she lost last month."

Tiffany leans back, crosses her arms and stares hard at Branson. "I didn't put it somewhere, you idiot."

Mrs. Spangler turns to Tiffany and pats her on the arm. "There there, dear. Nothing to worry about." She swivels back to Branson and there's none of the sympathy she showed her daughter two seconds ago. "I'd like to speak to Mr. Peabody immediately," she says in a hard voice.

"He's off today."

"Call him at home."

"I'm afraid he's unreachable. He'll be in tomorrow, however. I'd be happy to relay your message then."

Mrs. Spangler pauses to decide if she should keep throwing a fit, but even she can see that Branson is intractable. "Fine. You may have Mr. Peabody call on me at two o'clock sharp tomorrow afternoon. Not a minute late."

"But, Mom—" Tiffany's whining now, not wanting the confrontation to be over.

Mrs. Spangler shakes her head slightly. It's

enough to shut Tiffany up until she sees me at the other side of the counter, watching her.

"What do you want, homely?"

Mrs. Spangler turns and gives me the head-to-toe sweep like Tiffany did in the elevator last week. "A new friend of yours?" she says.

Mrs. Spangler and Tiffany laugh like they've both just heard the best joke ever. They walk off arm-in-arm to the elevators, whispering and laughing between them, stealing glances over their shoulders at me. I hear "She wore that ratty thing last week" and "God, she's pathetic, isn't she?" and "Why doesn't she comb her hair?" and "Did you ever see such black eyes? Terrible."

Branson walks over to me, a kind smile on his face. I see he has lots of places for piercings, but none in. Empty holes where shiny, pretty things should be. I think people like Mrs. Spangler probably make him keep them out. His collar almost covers his neck tattoo, but not quite. It's an intricate Celtic design that speaks of a patience Tiffany and Mrs. Spangler couldn't hope to understand. "Are you all right, miss?"

"I'm okay. Are you okay?"

Branson smiles and shows me his very white teeth. "Thank you for asking. Yes, I'm fine."

"My name is Lily," I say. I offer my hand to shake. I think we've bonded, Branson and me. We've both been harassed by the Spangler duo.

Branson envelopes my hand in both of his, squeezes, then lets go. "It was great meeting you, Lily."

I walk fast toward the glass doors. Before I get there, though, I turn back and give Branson a little good-bye wave. He's nice and I don't know if I'll see him again since Tiffany's mom might get him fired. He waves back and gives me another big smile. I think maybe I've made his day a little better.

I don't feel too bad about that.

I'm walking fast past the water fountain, late for my bus. The water's taking a break from all its dancing—quiet now, gone to its own nothing place.

"Hey, Lily!"

I turn toward the voice and see a familiar face. "Oh hey. Rick, right?" Not Rick. Nick. Like Andros. Anders.

His black hair waves back and forth when he shakes his head. He's got that surprised look on his face again. "Nick, actually." His expression says, *how could you forget my name?* His mouth says, "Still up for Pike's?"

I think about last week and try to remember if I said I would go to Pike's with Nick. I don't remember promising.

"Oh, sorry," I say. "Not today. I'm late."

Nick looks taken aback. I'm a little annoyed he's so sure of himself. Or me. Or girls in general. "Sorry," I say again and start walking toward the bus stop.

"Wait," Nick says. "We could still head down."

"I've got to get home."

"Not 'Aunt Margie's' anymore?"

"Sorry?"

"Last week you were calling your place 'Aunt Margie's.' This week you're calling it 'home.'"

"Yeah, okay." I'm uncomfortable with his scrutiny, his notice. I stare at him and wait.

"Come on. I won't keep you long, I promise," he says. The confidence is back. He's sure I'll say yes.

"I can't. I've got to catch my bus."

"How about I give you a ride home then?"

"No. That doesn't work for me."

He grins. "I've never met a girl so comfortable with the word 'no.'"

"Guess you have now." I turn toward the bus stop again. My bus is pulling away. "Crap."

"What's wrong?" Nick asks. He's sidled up beside me. I step away because he's too close.

"There'll be another one in half an hour," I mumble.

"Let me give you a ride home."

"No thanks, I'll wait."

Nick rolls his eyes. "Fine, then walk with me down to Pike's. I'll have you back here in time for your next bus." He presses his hands together and starts to walk backward, like playing cute will make me go. "Please."

"It's that close?"

"I walk there all the time." Nick's halfway down the big concrete steps leading away from Dr. Pratchett's building, grinning and beckoning with his hands. "Come on—no one can resist flying fish. Seriously, as far as fish throwers go, these guys are the best."

I already saw the fish throwers with Mom last summer, but I don't say this. I look around, trying to memorize where I am, making sure a not-Hank or real-Hank isn't following. I'll have to pay attention now.

I follow Nick like I'm a normal person shopping for some produce or a CD or a new scarf, maybe a tie-dyed T-shirt if I'm in the market. We walk into the main arcade and Nick goes right over to the flowers and buys a big bunch. I think his mom's sent him on a flower-getting mission until he hands them to me. They're Gerber daisies. He can't know they're my favorite.

"For you," he says.

I haven't caught up yet and say, "Won't your mom want those?"

"Um, I bought them for you." He's smirking now, giving me his lopsided grin.

I take the flowers. "Thanks."

"You don't like these?"

I look at some pomegranates in a box to my right. Bright red orbs with two bees buzzing around them. Not my buzz. Their buzz. "They're great, my favorite, actually. Thanks. Really."

"You're welcome." I look up at Nick when his tone turns shy. He's smiling like he's just won the lottery. I guess he thinks picking my favorite flower is a pretty amazing feat. Seems like his being shy is the amazing feat.

"Let's walk around a bit?" he says.

I hold the daisies close to me so they don't get crushed by the crowds. My hands are full between Dr. Pratchett's bag with the book that tells about my issues and Nick's daisies. We make our way down aisles of fruit and more flowers, Nick leading the way. There're a lot of people browsing, picking things up, putting things back down. I notice the mothers and daughters the most, how sometimes the kids are impatient when their moms try to get them to look at something, how they just want to be left alone with their cell phones and iPods. I want to tell them to spend the time and don't worry about how it looks to their friends. If they just spend the time maybe they won't regret so much later on.

Pretty soon we hear some guys hollering—the fish throwers. Nick's standing a little close, but I don't mind so much right now. We watch fish fly through the air and guys with rubber aprons laughing like it's the best time of their lives.

Nick pulls me away just as a wayward fish flies by.

"Sorry, kids!" one of the fish guys hollers. "Free fish for the lovebirds!"

Nick holds up his hand. "No thanks. We're fine."

We move on so we're not almost hit by more fish. Nick's arm is around my shoulders and I don't mind so much. He's warm and where he touches feels alive. It's the only place that does. My skin: alive from Nick's touch. There are no flutters inside, though. No room for nerves. All seats taken. "Thanks for pulling me out of the way back there," I say.

He drops his arm and says, "Guess you're lucky I was available, not off saving the world or something." Nick's chin is up, his chest out like he's going to show me the big S he's got painted there. "I've heard of people getting killed by flying fish."

"I think maybe you're full of it."

Nick gives me an exaggerated look of hurt. "You save a girl's life—"

"You saved me some laundry," I say and point at Mom's sweater.

Nick shakes his head. "So ungrateful."

There's easy silence between us as we head out to where the street performers and artists are selling their stuff. Nick stops at a musician's booth to look through some CDs. The guy pictured on the cover is sitting on a wooden stool a few feet away. He's holding an acoustic guitar and singing softly into the noisy crowd. I watch him and after awhile he watches me too. He's singing something I've never heard before. I'm listening to this guy with a long white beard who's wearing a hat I'm pretty sure I've seen on an old TV show—a panama or something—and he's singing about shouting down the wind. Shouting down the wind like he can make a difference. He doesn't get that something as constant as the wind can't be changed. Rain, lightning, wind, bullets—none of it can be changed. You can't shout down anything. You can't win.

I look away from the old guy with too much hope and see Hank standing behind him, watching me with his flat mantis eyes. Watching and waiting. His shirt is the same as what he wore at the bookstore—black button down. No jeans, though. Khakis this time. His work boots are the same, splattered with dried paint. He lifts one hand and waves. I think he tries to smile, but it's something else, something not right. His head tilts, his eyes roll to the side and I see he's busy listening again. Not to the music, though. Hank's listening to something else and by the look on his face it's something he doesn't want to hear.

Hank's whole face is frowning and he's turning away when Nick comes along and bumps my hip. "Wanna sit by the water?"

Light green, Nick's eyes, and full to the brim. He wouldn't agree with me about not being able to shout down the wind. I think inside Nick there's a lot of hope and happiness and sureness. Something behind it all too, I see now—something that makes me a little curious. I look back to where Hank or not-Hank was standing. He's gone now, disappeared into the crowd or thin air. I don't know which.

"Okay, then I have to go," I say to Nick.

We're walking toward the water and Nick's touching my back lightly with is fingertips and I feel that aliveness again—little dots of light even through Mom's sweater.

I stop a few feet behind a bench. This is where Mom and I sat when we visited last summer. The bench is where she told me our trip to Seattle wasn't a vacation, that she'd already contacted a lawyer. The bench is where she told me we were leaving Hank.

"You okay?" Nick is asking.

"I'm okay."

"Want to sit on that bench?"

I walk toward it.

Nick's laughs. "Guess that's a yes."

We sit down and I stare out at the water. Except for a few more boats in the harbor today, the scene is exactly the same. I remember my thoughts then—how big the water seemed, how infinite and unending. I wondered about the fishermen, how they didn't go crazy with just water around them, how they could stand the too-big quality of it.

Now I know different. Now I know there is no vast out there. It's like Margie's metal boxes, some heavy and small, some light and big, everything you think you know turned on its head. The vastness is when Hank came with his bullets and took Mom. The smallness is everything else. Even the ocean's a puddle.

Nick is speaking.

"Sorry, what?" I say.

"How are things going at your Aunt Margie's?"

"Fine." I'm busy shoving away thoughts about the day I came here with Mom. I'm thinking *Fish Throwers* and *Moby Dick* and *King book signing*. I'm thinking *Binka's whiskers*. The bees stay away, but the bench feels like a conduit. It's sending the memories right through me.

"Just 'fine'?" Nick's asking.

I glance at him and wonder if he sees me remembering. "This isn't my first time in Seattle." My words surprise me.

"Oh yeah?" Nick says. He doesn't know what else to ask, is probably afraid I'll start hacking again, coughing because I can't say the words.

I watch Nick's face and think about Mom's that day. The sunshine didn't let her makeup cover the bruise on her cheek and the white bandage over her stitches was bright against her creamy skin—reminders of Hank's year with Grandpa Henry, his growing rage, his hitting Mom a few days before we left for Seattle. I wanted to reach out, touch her cheek, tell her I'm sorry Hank decided to keep installing rain gutters after his year was up, that he thought Grandpa Henry was right after all. I wanted to tell her that I missed Dad too, that I wanted us to be a real family again. But then she said we were leaving for good and everything froze on my lips.

"Poor Lily, I knew her when she had a future bright with the promise of door management." Nick-the-joker's waving his hands at the water like he's talking to a crowd of people. "Now she's just another girl, sucked into an un-ambitious world, a world where lethargy is the only skill one needs, a world of..." He shakes his head, clasps his hands to his heart. "Bench warming." He purses his mouth and squints his eyes up like he's going to cry. "So much potential... wasted." He hangs his head dramatically and looks at me out of the corner of his eye. "You awake, Spacey?"

I give him a little grin. "I'm here."

He straightens up and scrutinizes me in that bright, curious way of his. "What's up?"

"I sat on this bench with my mom," I say before I can stuff it back inside, save it for Dr. Pratchett or Binka, who won't tell my secrets.

"When?" he asks. His voice is gentle now, all joking gone. That something behind his happiness, his lightness, is front and center now.

"A long time ago." A year, a lifetime.

"What happened? I mean, obviously something happened."

I run my fingers along the splintery space between me and Nick. "Here is where she told me we were leaving Hank."

"Is Hank your dad?"

Nod.

"Your parents are divorced." He doesn't ask, just assumes. His eyes say he understands me now, thinks I'm broken because my parents split up.

"She died," I say.

Nick is surprised. He turns his body toward me. "I knew there was something about you." He smiles a little and takes a deep breath. "My mom died too."

The something behind his eyes is right there in his frown now—recognition, familiarity, understanding, sadness. "I'm sorry," I say. "What happened?"

"She was sick for a long time. Cancer."

"Oh."

"What about your mom?"

Moby Dick.

"Hank."

King book signing.

"Shot her."

Fish throwers.

Nick takes in a big lungful of air. I'm looking at the daisies in my lap now, how the petals are a dark red and velvety and beautiful. His hand comes on over and covers mine up. Light and dark, mixed right there together. Our hands, the Yin and Yang now. His fingers are long, slender, and when he touches me, I jump a little. The sparks are so unexpected. Still no flutters, though. My skin knows about Nick, but the knot in my chest doesn't much care.

"Where is he now?"

I tilt my chin and gesture with my head because I don't want to move my hands. "Out there."

"He got away?"

"Yes."

"Were you...?" Nick waits, hoping I might fill in his question I guess. I don't know my lines or what he wants to ask.

"What?"

Nick pulls his hand away and swallows hard when I look at him. "Were you there?"

"Oh." Cloudy plastic, an arc of blood that says Mom lived but doesn't anymore. Little animal sculptures that tell more about Hank, about me, than I thought. Gouged plaster. Glass mosaics. "I was there."

There's a lot of quiet between us. Nick looks at me. I look at Nick. In his eyes I see understanding and fear. Always fear. I think as long as I live people will have that look when I tell them Hank came with his gun. They don't understand how a person could still talk, still *be* after that. I don't know either, but I think it has something to do with the bees and the hollow inside, with Margie and her boxes, Binka and her whiskers.

I look around for Hank, wondering if talking about him might conjure him up. He's nowhere. I think maybe it was a not-Hank standing behind the old guy with too much hope after all. Just another not-Hank in a city full of not-Hanks.

I look back at Nick, see words behind his expression, but none touching his lips. "You don't know what to say."

"Did he, um, hurt you too?"

I think telling Nick about Hank's kitchen bullets, his coming for me, isn't such a good idea. "No," I say.

We watch each other for awhile and I decide this might be awkward. "I'm sorry about your mom. Is your dad okay?"

Nick smiles a little. "Actually, it's my mom who's not okay."

I wait for him to explain.

"My mom—the one who died—is my bio mom. Her partner—wife—is my other mom."

"You have two moms?"

Nick nods. "And two dads. My dads are married to each other, so were my moms."

"That's a lot of parents," I say.

"Yep." He watches me, gauging my reaction. I don't know what he's looking for, what he wants me to say, so I tell him a little story.

"Mom and me, we lived next door to Mel and Bobby. We loved them. They were our only friends at the dog food house. Sometimes they came over for Mom's hamburgers or to borrow a cup of whatever, sometimes just to watch the sun go down."

Nick looks relieved, like he thought I might not understand about his parents. "They sound nice," he says.

"The best."

"Do you keep in touch?"

I shake my head. "I forgot to say good-bye even. I was sort of out of it."

"And that's different from now... how?" Nick's

grinning, all that light and happiness taking over again.

"Not so different now," I say.

"Thanks for understanding about my mom," he says.

"You miss her a lot."

Nick nods. "I do."

"Is it good you have your dads, your other mom, or are they too much sometimes?"

Nick looks at me twice—a double take. "Sometimes it's too much. How'd you know?"

"Even my Aunt Margie's too much for me sometimes." I smile like I'm joking because I feel bad, but it's true. Sometimes just Margie is too much. I think it's why the quiet place is nice, tempting.

Nick's mouth turns down. "You know what some of my friends said when Mom died?"

"No."

"They said 'well, at least you have spares.'"

"That's... um... wow."

"Yeah. I kinda ditched them because of it, which is why I'm spending a lot time down here this summer." He waves his arm toward the market.

"Do you miss them?"

Nick shakes his head. "That's the weird thing. I really don't. None of them understood what I was going through, you know? After a few months they expected me to be over it and back to the way things were. When I wasn't, they started hounding me." Nick looks at me, his eyes wide, unbelieving. "My best friend said I was dwelling on it too long. Believe that?"

I think about Hank in those last few months, how he would say the same thing when one of us got sick. *Malingering* was the word he used. He said if we weren't so lazy we'd get better faster. I remember when Mom had the flu so bad she needed to go to the emergency room, how I finally had to get a neighbor to take her because he wouldn't. Mom withdrew after that, starting to leave for work earlier, coming home later. It was the worst time for yelling and the start of when Hank accused her of awful things.

"I'm sorry your friends said that."

Nick nods. "It's nice to talk to someone who understands."

Bees come along and I think maybe they're not mine. I like being here with Nick, talking about our moms and I don't feel like going to the quiet place. I'm hoping there're one or two buzzing around, looking to fill up on daisy pollen from Nick's flowers, but there aren't. Only the ones inside my head. I think it's because Nick sees me—inside where I've gone. Right down into the hollow. I think also it's because I've spoken the words. I've told Nick what happened.

I wonder if now's a good time to answer the bees, the phone, to find out what it all means. When I think this, though, the bees buzz louder and I feel the quiet place wanting me.

"I'd better get back now." Bus. I need to catch my bus.

"I can take you home."

"Maybe another time." I stand up and gather my things. We head back the way we came in. I walk fast, hoping maybe if I hurry I might not go quiet in front of Nick. He knows about Mom. He knows about Hank. He doesn't need to know about me too, about the nothingness, about my mind slipping and sliding all over the place.

Pretty soon we're at the bus stop and the bus is at the curb. I need Binka. I need my tether. I pull out my cell phone, bring up her picture and stare at my kitten's face. "Thank you for the flowers," I say to Nick.

"Sure. Listen, can I have your number? To make sure you get home okay?"

I hand my cell phone over. "Can you put yours in here? I'll call you when I get to Margie's."

While Nick's programming in his number, the bees invite a few friends. While I'm stepping up the bus stairs, the friends invite friends. While I'm watching Hank weave his way down the long aisle toward me, his eyes looking left, right, then back at me, the hive takes over. Pretty soon I go where it's quiet. Right there on the bus with Hank coming toward me.

My cell phone's playing a tune. Margie's changed the song since the last time it rang—something upbeat, something you can tap your feet to. I pull it out of my pocket and open it. "Hello?"

"Lily?" It's Aunt Margie.

"Yes?"

"Are you okay?"

"I'm okay."

"Where are you?"

I look around. I'm still on the bus, at the back. There are people in their seats, facing forward. I don't recognize where we are. The bus doors are just whooshing shut, a bunch of used-to-be passengers standing on the sidewalk outside. Hank's in the middle of them, still with his black button-down shirt, his khakis instead of jeans, his black mantis eyes that aren't hurt anymore, just full of rage and decision. I don't smell whiskey or paint or mint.

"Lily?"

"I'm on the bus."

"Are you on your way home?"

"Yes. I fell asleep."

"Where are you?"

"Hold on."

I cover the phone's mouthpiece and tap on the shoulder of a woman sitting in front of me. "Where are we?"

"Near downtown," she says.

"How far from Queen Anne?"

She thinks for a minute. "Probably twenty minutes or so."

"Thank you."

"Sure."

I get back on the phone with Margie. "I'm about twenty minutes away, Aunt Margie. Are you at home?"

"Yes. I called a few times and came home when I couldn't reach you." Margie's voice is upset and scared.

"Sorry. I promise I'll be home soon."

"I'll watch for you. Twenty minutes."

I hang up and tuck my cell phone in my pocket. Dr. Pratchett's Twice Told Tales bag is on my lap now. I remember leaving it on the seat next to me and putting Nick's daisies on top of it. The daisies are still there, wilted from no water, velvety petals scattered on the seat and the floor underneath. I put my hand on Dr. Pratchett's bag, letting my fingers feel through the canvas, trying to understand why it's on my lap. I only feel the outline of the workbook inside.

I open it wide all at once, my insides leaping because I think maybe it wasn't a not-Hank I saw at

Pike's and on the bus and outside the window after all.

A picture is peeking out from where it's tucked behind the cover of the workbook that tells about my issues. I reach inside, pull it out slowly, but keep it face down.

I wait until we get to Queen Anne, wait with my hand shaking over the picture that shouldn't be inside my workbook. When we're still a block away, I ding the bell for my stop and turn the picture over at the same time.

Margie and me in Mom's meadow. A picture of our backs, of us sitting close together, waiting for a whisper, a *good-bye* to come along. Hank was there the whole time. In Mom's meadow where she was supposed to be safe.

Click. Snap.

I get off at my stop and take Nick's daisies, leaving a trail of petals from the bus down the block to Margie's apartment—bullet-shaped red petals that say I let them dry out, that I killed them.

Margie's waiting for me when I open the door. She's not mad. She's scared.

"Lily, what happened?" There's guilt too, like it's her fault I blanked out on the bus.

"I'm sorry I'm late, Aunt Margie."

She wraps her arms around me. "Where have you been?" Her voice is chock full of fear.

"I fell asleep on the bus."

"Lily, tell me the truth."

I scoop up Binka where she's sitting on the couch and hold her to my cheek. She puts her head under my chin and pushes hard.

"I went to Pike's with Nick—"

"Nick?"

"He lives in Dr. Pratchett's building. I met him on the elevator. He's nice." I sit down on the couch, Binka's head still pushing under my chin.

"How old is Nick?" Margie asks in a careful voice.

"My age."

Air whooshes through her white lips. "Okay. Why did you go to Pike's with Nick?'

"I missed the first bus. He invited me."

"And was today the first time you met him?"

"No—last week."

"Why didn't you mention him then?"

I look down at Binka where she's curled herself up in my lap. "I forgot."

"Lily," Margie says. "Did Nick do something to you?"

"No. Nick's nice."

"It's been two hours since you finished your session with Dr. Pratchett. Have you been with Nick this whole time?"

I look up at Margie and see she knows already. "I had a spell on the bus." I say. "I'm sorry."

She shakes her head. "Don't apologize for something you can't help. Just tell me the truth. Are you okay? Did anyone bother you?"

I think about the picture Hank left that tells me he's been with us the whole time, about him standing with a bunch of bus riders like he's a normal person touring the city. If I tell Margie, she'll send me away. To Mack and Darcy's. To the loony bin. Away from Binka.

"No, Aunt Margie, I'm fine. Everything's fine."

"I never should have let you go on the bus. I'm sorry," she says.

I hold out my arms and wrap them around her without disturbing Binka. "It's okay. Nothing happened."

Margie puts her hot face against my neck, her whole body shaking. "It's not me I'm worried about. My god, Lily. My god, if something *had* happened..."

"It didn't. It's a small thing, the bus. We can forget about it. We can let it go."

She sits up and looks hard at me. "You'll never go on the bus again."

"Okay."

"Never," Margie says again. "I'll take you every time."

"Your job, though."

"You're first, Lily."

Margie decides to invite friends over for a dinner party on Saturday. I'm expected to go. She says it's important I start meeting other people.

"I met someone, remember? I went to Pike's with him on Thursday? The flower guy? Nick?"

"I know and I think that's great, but I'd like you to meet my friends now. You're a big part of my life and they are too."

Margie's voice is unbending. I send out a little ribbon of hope that Hank will wait to come for me until after the party. I tell myself I don't feel afraid about Hank coming with this bullets, his decision, that there's no room inside for fear. All seats taken. I tell myself this, but when I look over at Binka sleeping on the couch and at Aunt Margie stuffing manicotti shells with a bunch of different cheeses, at all the metal boxes that mean different things, at the apartment that's starting to feel like home, I'm not so sure anymore.

"Tell me more about this Nick guy," Margie says.

"He lives where Dr. Pratchett has his office."

"I know. You mentioned that. What else?"

"He's nice."

She grins at me. "Well, good, I'm glad you're meeting people. You need to be careful when you do, though, okay?"

"I shouldn't have gone to Pike's?"

"No, I think it's great. I hope you'll let me meet this Nick soon. I just want you to be careful. Besides the episodes, you're a little spacey. Know what I mean?"

"I'm careful," I say. "Nick's a good person. He, um, he lost his mom too." My voice is so quiet Margie has to stop what she's doing and lean forward to hear me.

"And you told Nick about your mom?" she asks, her voice all hope.

"Yes. We sat on the bench where Mom told me we were leaving Hank. It brought back some memories. From when we were here before?"

Margie keeps her hands busy making manicotti, but I see she's tense and wants to ask more questions. Push, don't push. Pester, don't pester. "It was really nice when the two of you came last year," she says. Her voice is careful.

"Mom loved your apartment. I did too. You didn't have all the boxes, though."

Margie's eyes flit to mine, then back down to the manicotti. "I put them away when you came last time."

"Because they would've reminded Mom of Hank."

She nods.

"I'm glad you left them out now."

"I didn't have time—" She looks up, her eyes wide. She doesn't finish, doesn't need to.

"It's okay. I know you had to leave fast." I watch Margie stuff a couple more shells. "Thank you, by the way. For taking care of me."

Margie smiles a little. "Wouldn't trade it for the world." She wipes tomato sauce on her face when she brushes her cheek with a gooey finger. "I'm glad you had a nice chat with Nick."

"He's easy to talk to."

I watch Margie's fingers stuff cheeses like it's what she does for a living and wonder if she looks like this when she's making her boxes. Elegance and strength and care in Margie's hands, total concentration on her face.

"Do you know Nick's phone number?" she says.

"Why?"

"Well, if you're up for it, I think it would be nice to invite him over. That way you have someone familiar here and I get to meet your new friend."

I shake my head slowly. "I'm sure he has something to do."

"Up to you, kiddo."

"He's probably got a date or something."

"Wouldn't hurt to ask."

I think about going to Pike's with Nick and I don't mind the idea of him being here. "Okay, I'll call him," I say. "His number's in my phone."

Margie looks surprised and happy. She skips off to get my cell phone after she washes off her manicotti goo. She brings her laptop too.

"What's Nick's last name?"

"Andros. Wait, like Andros. Anders."

Margie looks completely confused.

"Anders."

She types quickly, then turns the laptop around so I can see what she's looking at—a bunch of pictures with "nick anders + seattle" typed into a search field. Clever Margie.

"Do you see him here?"

I see Nick's picture right away and point at the second one in the second row. "That's him."

Margie whistles. "He's gorgeous."

"Yeah, I guess."

She looks at me. "You do like him, don't you?"

"I think he's nice."

Margie shakes her head. "Good enough for me." She clicks on the picture, which goes to the website where it's posted. Pretty soon she's muttering under her breath, reading, "...scholastic achievement... first place state science fair... my god, Lily, he's brilliant. Did you know he's slated to graduate a year early and go to an ivy league college?" She reads a little more and her mouth drops open. "An ivy league college *of his choice?*"

Margie's looking at some high school site where Nick's got a page dedicated just to him. I get where his confidence comes from now. "No, I didn't know."

"Okay, kiddo. Time to use that thing." She points to the phone in front of me.

I don't feel nervous picking up the phone. I don't feel much of anything, but I do remember Nick's hands, the way they made my skin feel alive where he touched me. I find where he's programmed his number, dial him up. He answers on the second ring.

"Hi, Nick, this is Lily Berkenshire. From Pike's."

"Lily! You were supposed to call me yesterday when you got home."

"Oh yeah. Sorry, I forgot."

"Figures. Glad you called now, though." Nick's voice tells me he *is* glad.

"My Aunt Margie's having a dinner party tonight. We were wondering if you'd like to come. I understand if it's short notice."

"What are you having?"

"You get so many offers you have to decide where to go based on what's for dinner?"

Margie's hands are frozen, her mouth hanging open, eyes wide.

"That and who else is coming," Nick's saying, his voice all smiles. "Saturdays are usually reserved for fresh seafood. First choice lobster, second choice salmon. There should be at least one member of the Seahawks in attendance. Mascots don't count, just so we're clear."

"We're having manicotti and I have a kitten named Binka. Will that be good enough, your highness?"

Nick sighs.

"Five," I say. "Four. Three–"

"What are you doing?" he says.

"Counting down. This offer's good for another 1.8 seconds."

He laughs. "Oh all right, I guess I can make an exception. Can I bring something?"

I cover the mouthpiece, whisper to Margie, who's still shocked into frozenness. "Can Nick bring something?"

She shakes her head without closing her mouth.

"Just your sarcastic self, I guess."

"I can do that. Where do you live?"

I give him the address and directions, then grin at Margie's mouth opening even wider. When I hang up she just stands there looking at me.

"See, I told you Nick was nice," I say. I grin a little wider because I know Aunt Margie is happy I joked around with Nick, that I remembered the address to her apartment.

She finally closes her mouth. "He, um… that's great, Lilybeans. Really, really great." She goes back to her manicotti, a little smile on her lips.

"What do I say?" I ask because it occurs to me it's easy to talk to Nick and Dr. Pratchett and especially Binka, but sometimes I have a hard time with Margie. Maybe I'll have a hard time with her friends too.

She looks up from her work, squinting. I haven't used enough words again.

"To your friends." I roll my eyes, pretending I'm normal. "They'll think I'm a dork."

"No they won't. And they'll do most of the talking, believe me," she says. "Especially Sam. He's chatty."

"Is he your boyfriend?"

Margie snorts. "No. Sam's not into girls so much."

I think about this for a minute. "He's gay?"

She nods.

"Mel and Bobby lived next door to me and Mom. We loved them. Also, Nick has two dads and two moms. Well, one mom now."

Margie looks surprised. "Really?" She thinks on this a minute, then goes back to stuffing shells. I think she's planning to feed the neighborhood with all the shells she's stuffing. "Well, you'll love Sam too. He's a hoot."

"I didn't say good-bye."

"To Mel and Bobby?"

"Yes."

"I have no doubt they understand."

I think about Mel and Bobby for a little while. I wonder if they have new neighbors, if there are people in the dog food house again. I wonder if the new people have pictures on the walls and if they're watering the flowers Mom planted out front. I wonder if they use our old grill and if they taste cedar smoke in their burgers, if they've found the pot of gold and the splintered glass, if the plaster is still a crater or if it's plaster again. I wonder if they'll slice pineapple, if they've found Tiananmen Square.

In the dog food house. Where we were happy for a little while.

Margie wants to do my hair for the party. Binka follows me into the bathroom and curls herself up in the sink while I shower, then sits on the vanity and watches me comb out my hair after. Her whiskers twitch and I can see she wants to go full spaz in some impressive way. She hops off the vanity, goes over to the bathroom door and stares daggers at the handle. It's one of those lever types that goes up and down instead of twisty. She squishes her whole body to the floor, wiggles her butt, then springs with everything she's got. She wraps her front paws around the handle, hangs, swings. I can see she's trying to open the door, that with a few more pounds she'll be able to. Margie knocks and she drops back to the floor. She looks up at me, her whiskers twitchy, proud of her spaz achievement.

"What's that little beast up to?" Margie says out in the hall.

I hit the lever and let Margie in. "Trying to open the door by herself."

The kitten's taking a bath now, acting casual.

"You know I found her kibble in my best shoes the other day?" Margie says.

"Doesn't surprise me." I find Binka's food in my shoes all the time—on my pillow, under my covers too, on Margie's boxes, behind the bookcases. Little presents.

Margie looks at Binka. Binka looks at Margie. Staring contest. Margie looks away first. Binka goes back to cleaning her face, her ears a little taller. She won. She knows it.

"And that she meows at my door around midnight? Every night?" Margie says like she didn't just lose a staring contest to a spastic kitten.

"Nope."

"You know she's the craziest little beast I've ever met?"

"Yup."

She laughs, then makes me sit down on the closed toilet. My hair's got a natural wave, so Margie uses a big round brush and a hair dryer to straighten it.

"So tell me more about Nick," Margie says. She's got one of those fancy quiet hairdryers, so it's easy not to yell to make yourself heard.

"He's nice," I say.

Margie clucks her tongue. "Well that I already knew, Lilybeans. Tell me more. He's very handsome. And apparently very smart."

Nick's face swims up in my mind. "I like his eyes. I think that picture you saw is old. His hair sticks up all over now, like he's always running his fingers through it, petting himself or something."

This tickles Margie. "What else?" she says. "Is

he a bookworm like you?"

"I don't know."

"You don't know another thing about him?"

I think about our walk through Pike's, his goofy words. "He's funny. He keeps the bees away. A good tether." I don't mean to speak these words out loud.

Margie pauses with my hair straight out from my head. "A tether? That's a neat way of looking at it. Have you told Dr. Pratchett about your tethers?"

"I don't think so."

"Well, I bet he'd like to hear about them. Have you figured out what makes the bees come?"

"Han—I'm not sure, Aunt Margie." I barely resist the urge to smack myself. It's getting harder, keeping it all straight—the stuffing and the lying and the watching. I wonder how much longer I can do it without slipping up.

"You were going to say Hank?"

"Yes, you know, memories about him."

"You can tell me that, Lilybeans. You don't have to stop yourself."

"Okay."

"Do you want to talk about your dad?"

I shrug. "He never told me about when he was a kid. What was it like growing up with Grandpa Henry?"

"Well, he was consistent, I'll give him that. Overbearing, controlling, cruel, but consistent. I remember this one time…" Margie leans around and looks me in the eyes. "You sure about this?"

In my mind I see Hank on the bus, think how he sat next to me in public where anyone could see him, about the picture he left that says there are no safe places, not even Mom's hidden meadow. He's coming for me and a little part of me is starting to not want to go. I think it's time to know more about Hank. "I'm sure."

Margie nods and goes back to doing my hair. "I was seven, Hank five. My mother left us with him for a couple weeks when her mother died. She had to go back East to take care of the arrangements. We had never been alone with my father for more than an hour or two at a time, but we were old enough to understand it wouldn't be a picnic. We begged Mom to take us with her." Margie's hands still, but she keeps the hairdryer going. "I remember Mama saying she wouldn't be gone long and that we should be good kids and everything would be just fine. I'll never forget the dull look of grief in her eyes, the slow way she packed her suitcases, like her body weighed twice as much as it did the day before."

I know what Margie means. Sadness is a big thing to carry around, like Margie's little silver box that looks light but isn't.

"After she left, my father did too. He came home early the next morning reeking of alcohol and screaming for Mom. Hank and I climbed to the attic and hid there until that afternoon. When the house had been silent for a long time and I couldn't hold my pee anymore, we went downstairs."

Margie turns off the hairdryer and leans against the vanity. Her mind is back in time, there with Grandpa Henry and his meanness.

"My father was sitting at the kitchen table, his hands clasped in front of him. He wasn't eating or drinking or reading. He was just sitting there, still, like he'd been waiting for us the whole time. When I saw him, I peed myself right there in the kitchen. He made me clean it up, gave us both brutal whippings with his favorite belt and put us to bed for two days. We were allowed to get up to use the bathroom and to eat one meal a day. The routine over the next two weeks was school, home, bed, start all over again the next day. And still only one meal. Our clothes were falling off by the time our mother got home."

I'm staring hard at Margie's face, seeing the hungry little girl in her, the scared daughter of a tyrant. But I'm thinking about Hank, how he controlled everything we did after he went to work for Grandpa Henry. Except for the food thing. He let us eat, but he drove away all our friends and he pressed our world into a tiny box. "That's what Hank did to us."

Margie's eyes come back, the hurt from her past making them bright and dull at the same time. "Your mom told me. I tried to talk her into leaving earlier, but she'd promised your dad a year?"

Nod. A year. One year to ruin everything.

"I'm surprised he let you go."

"Mom didn't give him a choice. She told him before he got to his whiskey. He yelled a lot, but I think he knew even before Mom told him. His year was up. We left that night before he started drinking. Drove all the way here."

Margie brushes my cheek with her fingertips. "I loved your mom like she was my own sister."

"She loved you too," I say because I'm sure it's true even though Mom didn't talk about Margie a lot. I think she kept Margie for herself.

We don't say anything more because the memories, the pain, they're like the kitchen window at the dog food house after Hank's bullet shattered it. Fragments that used to be whole, but aren't anymore. We don't say anything because sometimes silence is better than the pain.

When Margie's finished shining me up, she says I should wear some of the new clothes she's bought for me. Mom's sweater is on a hanger in the closet and I want to wear it like I sometimes want to use people as tethers. My touchstone, Mom's sweater.

"I'll try," I say.

"Now, how about some makeup?"

"Nah. I don't mind going as myself to this thing. Okay?"

Margie gets this amazed look on her face. "That's more than okay, Lilybeans." There's quiet between us and in Margie's half-smile, in the silence of this small bathroom, I realize something I didn't before. There's hope and love when people stop talking, when stillness takes over. It's a whole different kind of quiet place I didn't know about.

Binka's closed off in my room so she doesn't use Margie's friends as trees. The kitten's manners aren't the best and I don't have the heart to tell her different. Margie says we'll let her out when we're finished eating.

I'm sitting on the couch, waiting and not waiting for the doorbell to ring. Everything inside me is leaping and thumping and rushing to the surface. Margie's shining me up, making me look pretty on the outside, doesn't change what Hank did, what he's doing now. It doesn't change Hank's picture inside the workbook. Doesn't change that I have a last letter from Mom, who loved me better than anyone and died anyway. Making my hair pretty, buying me new clothes, trying to fit me into this life—these things don't change the hollow, the bees, the not-Hanks and the Hanks. New quiet places don't change a thing.

I get up to tell Margie I can't do this, can't be with whole people, when the doorbell rings. She runs right for it and sweeps the door open before I can get a word out.

"Lily, this is Sam," Margie says, inviting him into the living room.

The thumping, the leaping, the rushing in me all slows down when Sam walks in. Right off it's easy to see why Margie wants him here. His eyes are so full of light it's like he's got his own personal fireflies right there behind the blue irises, flitting back and forth, shining everything inside up so it dances out to the person looking at him. He's big—height-wise and width-wise, blond and super goofy. His hair goes twenty different ways at once and I see it's intentional, not like how Nick pets himself. I don't think Sam would dare touch his hair. It's hard to imagine how long he spends in front of the mirror.

"Miss Lily Berkenshire," he says. "I've heard so much about you. Come, sit with me, tell me your story." Sam holds out his hands, whisks me to the couch. Margie's grinning and I'm mesmerized. We sit down and he folds an ankle under one leg, curling into himself a little. "I hear you like to write, Lilykins. Tell me more."

Everything in me settles and I find myself talking with Sam like I've known him my whole life, like I'm a regular person with plenty to share. It's easy to tell him about my journals, about how I haven't written in awhile. He doesn't demand anything and he doesn't ask about stuff that makes the bees come around. A perfect tether—Sam.

He leans forward and whispers conspiratorially. "Can I just say, Lily? You are gorgeous."

I look down at the T-shirt and shorts I'm wearing, at Mom's sweater over them.

Sam follows my gaze. "Okay, you could use some new clothes—"

"She has some," Margie yells from the kitchen.

"Well, Marge, next time help the girl dress proper. You know better." He winks at me while Margie makes a funny noise.

I feel the corners of my mouth tug up. "She tried," I say.

"Girl didn't try hard enough," Sam says real loud.

Margie makes another noise that's a little ruder than the first.

"Now, listen here, girl. I see you hiding yourself in those too-big clothes. It's time you took your aunt up on some wardrobe advice. What do you say?"

I find myself nodding, agreeing right away. "Okay."

Sam looks satisfied with himself. "Good. Now, tell me more. Tell me about that kitten you found, what, in a garbage can or some such?" His nose wrinkles up like he smells the old coffee grounds and banana peels.

I launch into every little thing Binka's done and find talking about my kitten is easy. He's nodding in all the right places and seems truly interested. Then he looks around the apartment with a perplexed expression on his face. "Where're you hiding this freaky little Tasmanian Devil?"

"Away," Margie calls from the kitchen. "She's a menace to our dinner."

Sam spends the next little while chiding Margie for her cruel ways. He even clucks his tongue at her. I almost laugh, but catch myself. I remind myself crying and laughing are right there together, and if I start one, the other might come along. Also, I don't want the bees here now, don't mind feeling like a regular person with everyday stuff to talk about.

"And what's this about a boy you've invited over?" Sam asks when he's finished teasing Margie.

"How'd you know?"

Sam waves his hand in the air. "Magic." He grins and winks. "Margie and I have a terrible habit of texting each other everything. We could write a book with our ridiculous little notes. Tell me about him."

"She doesn't know a whole lot!" Margie calls from the kitchen.

Sam jumps a little and sticks his tongue out in her direction.

"I saw that!" Margie hollers.

"He's nice," I say.

"Told you!"

"Hush, girl," Sam calls back. "Lily, there's got to be more than 'he's nice.'"

"He's good looking. Funny. Sarcastic."

Sam looks exasperated. "What's the boy's name?"

"Nick."

He cocks his head to one side, his eyes looking left, brow creased. "A good name," he says slowly. I think he's going to ask a question when the doorbell rings.

"They're here," Sam says in a dramatic, creepy voice. "To be continued." He smiles at me, pats my hand and heads on over to the front door, opening it right up. He doesn't look through the peephole, doesn't know about real-Hank out there with his picture-taking, his waiting, his plans from his dead father. I cross the living room, ready to jump in front of him if it's Hank. Sam's blocking the doorway, his shoulders too broad for me to see around.

"Nicky?"

"Sam!"

Sam looks back at me with his mouth open. "*This* is your Nick?" He breaks into the biggest grin I've seen on him yet.

I stand on my tiptoes and look over Sam's shoulder at Nick. "He's not mine, but he is a Nick."

Sam looks at Nick looking at me. "Oh, he's yours, sweetie, you just don't know it yet." He pivots out of the way and ushers Nick into the apartment.

My head is spinning and I can't figure out what's going on. "How do you know each other?"

"Sam and Dad dated before I was born, before Dad met Preston—my other dad. They're good friends still," Nick says.

Sam waves his words away. "We were always more friends than anything else."

"Not what I heard," Margie sing-songs from the kitchen.

Nick sees I'm still confused. "How I know Sam—he and Dad have been doing this book club thing at my house since I can remember."

"A book club?" I say. "That sounds interesting."

"Boring, actually," Nick says. "It's all nonfiction, political junk."

"You have to be involved to change the world, Nicky," Sam says, but he's got his usual big grin on.

Nick leans my way, rolls his eyes and whispers, "Dad's words."

"I thought you lived with your mom?" I say, still not catching up.

"We all live together, actually." Nick smiles. "It's a big apartment."

Sam's looking at Nick and there's this—something—besides the fireflies in his eyes. Something that makes his mouth half-smile. I remember the same expression on Mom's face after I got an A on a short story I wrote for English. She took that story to work and read it to all her friends over lunch. Pride. Pride is what I see in Sam's expression.

Sam leans toward me, his whole face grinning. "Anyhoo, Nicky is great, Lily. You have my blessing."

"As if she needs it," Margie says from behind me.

Nick laughs, looks embarrassed and shuffles his feet. I feel bad for Nick, decide he could maybe use a rescue from Margie and Sam and their big assumptions. "Nick thinks we should be having lobster and entertaining a Seahawks guy," I blurt. I decide I'm not good at this joking thing when Nick and Margie and Sam turn to stare at me. Then I decide maybe I am when Sam turns slowly back to Nick and slaps him on the arm.

"Cheeky monkey. I'm telling your dad."

Nick shrugs and grins, but doesn't look embarrassed anymore. "I thought it was the least Lily could do after I showed her around Pike's."

"You took this beautiful girl to that fish-infested hippy market and you want—" Sam looks to me again. "What did you say? Lobster and the Seahawks?"

"And he didn't care about Binka."

Mock horror. Sam doesn't say anything, just shakes his head until Nick's grinning so big all his teeth are showing. Sam finally turns around and shuffles off to the kitchen like someone's told him the worst news ever, all slump-shouldered and muttering to himself.

Margie's holding out a hand for Nick to shake. "It's great to meet you, Nick."

"You too," he says.

Margie closes the front door and heads back to the kitchen, leaving me and Nick standing in the living room alone.

Nick opens his arms wide. "Do I get a hug?"

There's something going on in my stomach, something like the hollowness I feel in my whole body most of the time. I want to step into Nick's arms, to feel his heartbeat against my ear, but I can't make myself do it. He's waiting and his grin is slipping and pretty soon his arms slip too.

"I'm sorry," I say. "I can't right now."

Nick nods. "It's okay. Don't worry about it." Like someone flipped a switch, he's smiling again, letting his hurt feelings go. I wonder how he does it. "You look different." He lets his eyes do the roving. "Your hair maybe?" Plops his hands on his hips, looking even closer. "Sweater's the same. No nose job, weird implants or piercings. Guess it's the hair."

"It's the hair," I say. "Margie did it."

"Very nice," he says.

Nick and me, we watch each other awhile. The light and happiness are there, but he's trying to figure me out too. If he was a cat, his ears and whiskers would be all the way forward. His eyes would be big, round and knowing. Nick sees down into the hollow without even looking hard. I don't know why he wants to be here with an empty girl, especially when he's got two dads, a mom, Sam, probably a bunch of other people. Nick's all wrapped up in love.

"Want to see the rest of the apartment?" I say because right now I don't want him trying to figure me out.

Before he can answer, Binka starts crying in my room. I hear Sam begging Margie to let him "fetch the poor little wretch."

I lead Nick toward the kitchen. "You don't know what a beast she is," Margie's saying when we get there. "You know she puts her food in our shoes? We let that gremlin out, you'll have to tie down anything you want to keep, including dinner."

Sam rolls his eyes. "Margie, Margie, Margie. The Drama. I know you can't possibly think a baby kitten is a threat to your epicurean masterpiece—"

"Sweet talk won't work," Margie says. "She can join us after dinner."

As if Binka's heard the finality in Margie's tone, she stops meowing. I imagine her curled up on my pillow, spreading her spaz fur all over the place.

Margie turns to Nick and me standing at the island now. "Nick, please excuse our chaos." She throws a look over her shoulder at Sam sinking his teeth into one of Margie's from-scratch loaves of French bread.

He turns around with an innocent expression and some bread crumbs down the front of his shirt. "What?" he says when Nick and Margie laugh.

With all the people here it's worse than I thought. I don't know what to say or how to act. Margie's friends are drinking wine and laughing and I'm watching them closely. They're all so normal and I think if I can mimic that more often, maybe I can stop Margie worrying. If I can just make my mouth smile and lift my arms in the air now and then for emphasis, maybe then the sad looks will stop.

I think you have to have something inside to pull it off, though. Like Sam has his fireflies and Margie's best girlfriend Jenny has her twinkle when she looks at her boyfriend Derek. Margie's all lit up inside too, so lifting her arms is second nature. Nick is happy, from his toes to his head. He joins in the conversation like he's known everyone forever, joking and laughing and teasing.

I feel like nothing but a tin girl with a few tethers that keep me from ripping open and dissolving. Nothing but tin and hollow and I don't remember how I was before. Hunted by Hank. Not normal anymore.

Mom always said I could see ahead of time how things will fit. I can't see how I'm going to fit into this life. These new people with their happiness—no potato bugs in their lives. No dog food. No tin. No fragments or cracks or spells. Just people being people.

I shake my head, trying to loosen these tight thoughts, these beliefs that I'm nothing more than an empty person who's sure enough getting filled up with not-Hanks and bees and pretty soon a big quiet that will leave me staring into space forever.

Nick touches my arm where he's sitting next to me at the dinner table. "Want to watch the sun go down?" He points at the door leading out to the patio. We're finished with Margie's manicotti and the French bread she managed to keep Sam from eating before Jenny and Derek got here.

"Sure," I say because maybe with just Nick I can say something besides nothing.

Margie smiles when I tell her where we're going. "Come back for dessert in a little while?"

Nick and me, we stand side-by-side at the edge of Margie's patio, leaning against the railing, looking out over the emerald city turning pink and red with the setting sun. Nick bumps my arm. "Your aunt's a good cook."

I keep watching the sun. "Here it comes," I say.

"Here what comes?"

"There's this moment of complete stillness at dusk," I say. "Like the whole world rests for just that second." Mom's words in my throat because she taught me about the dusk.

Nick glances at me, then back to the sunset. "I

never noticed."

"My mom showed me. At the dog food house it was when the tops of these huge trees behind the factory lit up orange and red."

Nick doesn't say anything, just keeps watching the sun go down.

"First the sky behind the trees would go yellow. Gold I guess you could say." My voice is a whisper because the stillness is almost here. "Pretty soon there was some orange and red mixed in. We'd get excited for the quiet like little kids on Christmas morning."

"Where's the moment here?" Nick asks. His voice is a whisper too, I think because he feels it coming. The stillness at dusk is big, unmistakable when you know about it.

"Here, it's when the whole city goes orange."

Nick reaches over and takes my hand. I squeeze it tight. Together we wait for the moment. "Here we go," I whisper. The sun's orange glow descends over the tall buildings first, down their sides, right across the earth like someone's turned on a big lamp. Not an explosion of light, nothing so dramatic. A peaceful blanketing where everything's lit, glowing, silent.

I'm here with Nick, but I'm thinking about Mom's eyes and how they'd go extra bright when the trees behind the dog food factory would light up orange and red, how everything would stop for just that moment. At the dog food house I couldn't hear the factory or the noisy kids down the block or even my own breath. At Margie's I can't hear the traffic or the wind or the next-door neighbor's chimes.

Red and orange and stillness.

And then it's gone.

I glance over at Nick. He's staring at me with a lopsided grin on his face.

"What?" I say. "Now you think I'm a dork?"

He only shakes his head and keeps grinning.

His grin is infectious and pretty soon I'm smiling right back. "What?"

"I'm glad I came over tonight."

"Even though there was no lobster?"

"I survived," he says.

I point over my shoulder. "There's dessert in there. Maybe that will make up for there not being a Seahawks guy here."

"Maybe," Nick says. He's still grinning, staring, and pretty soon I'm feeling a little squirmy, like Nick's realized something and he's not telling me what it is. I want to ask him what he's thinking again, but the door opens behind us before I can.

I let go of Nick's hand and turn to see who it is. Sam's standing there with Binka on his shoulder, his goofy grin plastered in place. "This baby was wasting away," he says. He's holding a little dish of ice cream and pretty soon he raises his spoon to share with Binka. She licks it daintily, but keeps her eyes on me.

"I know that look," I say, pointing at my kitten. "She's ready to go full spaz. We better get inside."

We head back in where Margie's dishing up ice cream and Derek and Jenny are sipping from big glasses of red wine. Nick and I stop at the kitchen island and wait for Margie to hand us some scoops.

Jenny comes up beside me, leans in close and asks me how I'm liking Seattle. I smell wine on her breath and flinch. The smell is up my nose. It's filling my head and everything's come back. All the nights of drinking. All the yelling. All the phone calls. All the old times, before things were good for a little while.

"You okay, Lilybeans?" Margie's voice is distant.

Everyone's quiet, looking at me, gathered in the

kitchen and silent. Now Nick will see where I go, see that watching a sunset and holding my hand won't make me a new girl. This hollow, these bees, they're my life now.

"Did you know she's hiding money?"

"Did you know you're poor for nothing?"

"Did you know she's sleeping with every guy she meets? Did you know your mother's a slut and a whore? Did you know, Lily, did you?"

"Lily, you know you can't do that, right? You know you aren't capable, that you don't have the intellect?" Dad's asking me this in his soft, low voice, his mean voice, his voice that tells me some part of him is enjoying what he's saying. It's just before we left, when Hank wasn't Dad hardly at all anymore. Grandpa Henry's voice was in Hank's throat all the time by then. Whiskey every night, Mom making plans I didn't know about. Our lights flickering more and more.

Mom's holding me in her arms on the couch. She's pressing my face to her chest like she can shield his words going into my brain, like she can make me think something different. "Shut up, Hank. She can do anything she wants. Lily, don't listen. If you want to be a writer, be a writer. You are brilliant."

I hear my father laugh like this is the funniest thing he's ever heard. "Brilliant? Brilliant, Rachel? Are you serious? The girl can barely pass math. She can barely get through a history test for god's sake."

"Get out, Hank. Go to the bar. Do what you have to do to get this meanness out. Leave our daughter alone."

I hear Dad launch himself from his barcalounger. Mom doesn't flinch. I unbury my hot, wet face and turn toward him, ready to scratch his eyes out if he touches my mother. He leans over, pointing a finger at her. I smell it on his breath—the booze, the stuff that lets him be as mean as he wants. "Don't you speak to me that way, Rachel. You know better."

"Get out," Mom says in her softest voice. "Please

just leave us alone for a little while. You say such cruel things. She's our daughter, our beautiful daughter. Don't you see the damage you're doing?"

My father straightens and looks down at me, down into my brown-black eyes with his little chips of cold onyx. "Sometimes I think she's too stupid to be my daughter."

My eyes flood again and I know he's right. I am stupid. It's been almost a year of Grandpa Henry in Dad's throat and I still cry when he says these things. The fact that I hurt so much proves his point. I don't learn too well.

Dad stomps out of the house and Mom tries to undo the damage. We both know there isn't a thing she can do to pull back the words, to make them different or not true. They slip right into the open cuts left by a father who used to love me, but hates me now. His words, they slip in like poison and they infect my blood and I live down to his expectations. I believe him.

"Lilybeans, come back to us," Margie's saying.

I blink once and then again. "I'm here, Aunt Margie."

She's sitting on my bed, holding my hands. I'm in my room with no idea how I got here, kneeling at my bed like I'm getting ready to say some random prayer. I feel Binka on my back, her tiny arms as far around my neck as she can stretch. She's got her nose pressed into my hair. Someone's making noise behind me and pretty soon Sam's sitting on my bed too. I'm flanked, pinned.

"How long?"

"Only a few minutes," Margie says.

"Okay."

Margie's eyes have pain. Sam's are serious now. I focus on Sam.

"You okay, Lilykins?" he asks like I've fallen off my bike and he's trying to keep me from crying. Casual-like he asks if I'm okay.

"Do you have any kids, Sam?"

He shakes his head.

"Do you want kids?"

"Very much. My partner Jason and I want to adopt, but there are... obstacles to overcome."

"If you ever have a kid, even if the kid isn't the brightest bulb in the pack, don't tell them that, okay? Don't tell them they're stupid."

Sam's eyes go extra bright and I hear Margie let out a big breath like she's been holding it for hours.

Sam reaches out a hand and touches my cheek gently with his fingertips. "Never," he says. "I hope, someday, I get to have a daughter like you, Lily. You are very special."

I feel surprised. Sam wants a tin daughter? A kid who's buried deep? Surprise is better than feeling all twisted up inside, so I take it.

"I know you don't believe me," Sam's saying. "It's okay. I think someday you will."

"How?" I ask because I can see he really does know.

Margie squeezes my hands and says, "One thing you'll notice as you get older is that we all recognize the hurt in each other when we've been through it ourselves." She brushes the sweaty hair off my forehead. "Sam sees in you some of his own experiences. And, what happened tonight—we all have triggers. For me, it's when I think someone's angry with me. Like if Sam jokes that my dinner tastes like crap, I think about how my father said the same thing to my mother, and I overreact. You understand?"

Sam nods. "For me it's yelling. Even just shouting from one room to the other. Like your Aunt Margie did when she was in the kitchen cooking dinner and we were chatting on the couch? It takes a lot for me not to bolt out of a room when someone's hollering."

"I smelled wine on Jenny's breath. It reminded me of Hank and his whiskey."

Margie and Sam exchange a look over my head, then glance behind me. I turn around, see Nick standing in the doorway.

"I go away sometimes," I say.

He nods, but I can see he's not so sure about me anymore. I can see he's thinking he's in over his head.

"It's okay if you want to go. I understand."

A little grin touches his mouth. "And miss the lobster? No way."

I try to smile back, but all I can think about is how these new people with their wholeness, their happiness, can't understand the bees, the not-Hanks, the hollow inside me. Nick tries with his joking, makes me think maybe I was funny once. Margie tries by explaining about her metal boxes, about how it was for her and Hank growing up. Sam doesn't try at all. He's just Sam, not a bit afraid to be who he is. And I think about how there's empty quiet in me just waiting to get filled up with something, maybe something closer to Hank than Mom if the bees have their way.

I try to let these thoughts go so we can salvage Margie's party. "I'm sorry I ruined everything."

Sam scoffs and tussles my hair. "You haven't ruined a thing, Lily. Not a thing." He plucks Binka off my back and sets her on his shoulder. "This baby is yet again wasting away. I believe she could do with a drop of kitten food."

When we go out to the kitchen, Jenny and Derek are getting ready to go. I tell Jenny I'm sorry and she gives me a big hug, says she understands. When she pulls back, I notice a scar on her face that runs from the middle of her cheek to the corner of her mouth. I think about what Margie said about hurt seeing hurt and wonder what happened to her. I don't ask, though. I just say good-bye.

Pretty soon Sam's feeding Binka some leftover cheese he found in the fridge and Margie's scolding him for creating a monster he doesn't have to worry about.

Nick looks at his watch and says he'd better get home after all, then asks me to walk him out. We head down the long path from Margie's front door to the curb out front. Nick points out his car where it's parked across the street, his face proud. It's an old car, a Mustang I think. He tells me the year, but I can't remember, can't think of anything but how Nick knows about Mom, Hank, my spells. The only thing he doesn't know is that I see not-Hanks too. I decide to keep that little gem to myself.

We're standing at the curb and Nick's smiling at me. "I was wondering if you'd see a movie with me tomorrow night."

I don't say anything, don't know what to say. Here I'm expecting Nick to say good-bye for good and he's asking me out. "What movie?" I finally ask.

"You get so many offers you have to decide whether to say yes based on what's playing?"

"That's right."

"Well, I don't know if you're into horror, but—"

"My favorite," I say before I can keep my mouth shut.

"Mine too," he says. "Well, there's an indie theater over by the university showing that one with the guy?"

"I'm supposed to know what movie you're talking about by that description?"

"Come on, I guess your favorite flower twelve seconds after meeting you, least you can do is read my mind."

"Does it have zombies?"

Nick's eyes go wide. "Seriously, are you psychic

or did you actually read my mind?"

"I don't tell my secrets," I say, then decide I need to work on my jokiness. "I mean, it's a secret." Truth is, Margie and I spent half an hour last night trying to find a good movie to see. She likes romance. I like horror. We couldn't decide. But when I saw the zombie movie listed, right off I wanted to go.

"So, you want to see it?" Nick says.

Where my heart used to be is pounding. *Thump-crack, thump-crack.* I don't understand Nick. He's seen me—really seen me. I don't know what he wants from me.

Finally, I look up from my shuffling feet. "What do you want from me?" I say. My voice, chock full of anger and I don't know why. Nick's been nothing but nice to me. "Why do you want to spend time with me? I'm broken inside, spacey like you said, maybe going crazy."

Nicks laughs a little. "You aren't going crazy." He tries to take my hand, but I pull away from him.

"How do you know?" I'm ready to go back into the apartment, forget this whole thing with Nick, this new life Margie wants me to fit into. All of a sudden I want the bees here, an excuse to go into the quiet place. These new people with their happy lives. I don't think I can take it.

Nick tucks his hands in his pockets and pulls his shoulders up. He's not smiling anymore. "I've never told anyone this, but after my mom died, I spent a lot of time away from the house. My parents thought I was with my friends. My friends thought I was at home. I'd go to this park and just sit on a swing by myself." He looks down at the sidewalk, then back up at me. "I'd be there for hours, just spacing out. I never had any idea how much time passed until my phone rang or the sun went down or it started raining and I came out of it."

"What were you thinking about?"

"Nothing. Hours would go by and I couldn't remember a single thought. I was just checked out, I guess. I never had anyone die in my life except my grandpa when I was, like, ten, you know? And when it's your mom or your dad, it's way worse than a grandparent. It's like you lost part of what made you you." Nick looks down at his feet again. "That doesn't even make sense."

I reach out and touch his arm. "It makes sense."

He smiles and pretty soon his light is back, shoving away the darkness. He points behind me, up the walkway to Margie's front door. "When we were looking at the sunset?"

I nod.

"That's when I knew."

Thump-crack, thump-crack for a whole different reason. "Knew what?" I don't like the tremble in my voice.

"You get things like other people don't. I never noticed that stillness thing you were talking about, but it was totally there. I think we see things differently now, you know? Like we notice things other people don't, maybe the stuff that's important."

We're quiet for a little bit, shuffling our feet, looking everywhere but at each other.

"I know you've got a lot going on right now," Nick finally says. "I was just hoping we could hang out, maybe watch a bunch of zombies get their heads chopped off. And I still owe you that personal fish, so we definitely have to hit Pike's again."

"Maybe I could call you tomorrow?" I watch my sneakers, feel my cheeks glowing bright. "Tonight was um... hard."

"Yeah sure," Nick says. "Movie's at eight, so

anytime before then."

Finally I glance up. "Okay. Talk to you tomorrow then?"

Nick nods, steps off the curb and crosses to his car. He turns before getting in, giving me a little wave and a big smile. "Don't worry about tonight, Spacey. I'd be way more worried if you weren't a little loopy after everything you've been through." He circles one finger next to his ear to make his point.

I grin in spite of myself, feeling amazed by Nick. I can't imagine him sitting on a swing at some park, spaced out and not knowing how much time has passed. Can't imagine him anything but whole and happy.

Sam's leaving when I get back to the apartment. He gives me a big hug, a smack on the cheek and tells me to make sure Binka gets enough to eat.

When I slip back into the apartment, Margie's sitting on the couch. She pats the cushion next to her, asks me to join her.

"What did you and Nick talk about for so long?"

"He asked me to a movie tomorrow night."

She grins. "What time?"

"I don't know if I want to go."

"Oh yeah?"

"Yeah." I look up from where I've got my hands clasped in my lap. "I told you Nick's mom died?"

She nods.

"I guess I don't understand..."

"You don't understand how Nick can still be

okay?"

Nod.

"Well, a lot of it has to do with time, but even more, it has to do with letting the people who love you help."

"You mean like his other parents?"

"Yes. Sam told me a little about Nick when the two of you were on the patio. I guess he had a very tough time when his mother died. It took about three months before he would talk about it with anyone. Once he did, though, Sam said he started feeling a lot better."

"I didn't feel better when I told Nick about Mom."

"I know. For you it's a little different. Nick's mom was sick for a long time and they didn't expect her to survive. Of course you're never ready, but Nick and his family had time to prepare." Margie squeezes my hand. "You're dealing with a whole lot more, kid. And you're dealing with it beautifully."

I look at Margie twice—a double take. "Beautifully? Aunt Margie, I hear bees in my head. I couldn't even talk to your friends."

"Uh-huh. And you made a friend within your first few days in Seattle—a cute, very smart boy who wants to take you to a movie. You charmed Sam so much he's begging me to let him show you the city." She points at Binka stretched out in the chair by the patio windows. "And you saved a kitten from a dumpster. Point is, you have more strength than you think you do. Remember what your mom said in her letter? Every word is true. It's hard to fathom now, I know, but I hope someday you'll see what everyone else does."

I want to tell Margie about the not-Hanks, to see if she still thinks I have strength and bravery like Mom said. I keep quiet, though, decide my aunt thinking I'm strong is better than the alternative.

She nudges me. "So, you think you'll go tomorrow?"

Nick and his movie invitation. I think about him sitting on the swing, checking out for hours at a time because he couldn't be around people, then waking up one day and deciding he could. I guess Nick understands more than I thought and he's still a good tether. I like being with him, I guess is what it comes down to.

"Yeah, probably," I say, which makes Margie smile.

I call Nick the next day and say I'll see the zombie movie with him, which makes Margie happy. I decide to wear some of my new clothes, which makes Sam happy when Margie texts him the news. Everyone is happy.

Me, I'm nervous like last night at the dinner party, but at least I know my voice will work with Nick.

Margie thinks I should spritz some of her expensive perfume on, so I tell her Nick will be here any minute and I'll wait for him outside. I close the door on Margie laughing, Binka shaking on her shoulder.

I walk down the long path from the apartment to the curb, not thinking about much of anything except how Nick doesn't think I'm crazy. His believing this has stuck with me and made me wonder if maybe Margie's right about there being more strength in me than I believe. Dr. Pratchett thinks I should answer the bees, Mom thought I was brave, Margie thinks I'm strong, Sam wants a daughter like me. Maybe there is more in me than nothing. Maybe I can answer the bees and not dissolve. Maybe answering the bees will make the not-Hanks go away. A lot of maybes, stuff to think about.

I stop at the curb and look down at the sneakers Margie bought me. They're grungy, worn-looking, chocolate brown. Perfect sneakers for a sticky movie theater floor. I hear a squeak and then a car door slam, but I keep watching my new-old sneakers.

Pretty soon paint-splattered work boots stop next to me. I still don't look up, deciding to ignore what I hope is a not-Hank. There's no whiskey, no mint, no paint, just the sweet summer air all around me.

"Hello, Beans."

"Go away."

"Can't do it, kiddo."

I look up at Hank, at his flat mantis eyes, at his mouth twisted into a frown. He doesn't look angry, just unhappy. "What do you want?"

He smiles and it is worse than the frown. "It's not what I want that's important, Beans. What's important is what *you* want."

Here's Hank, my used-to-be father who's gone crazy, and I don't know what he expects me to say, so I don't say anything.

"You want to come back and live with your dad again, don't you? You never wanted to leave in the first place, isn't that right, Beans? Your mom forced you."

I still don't say anything, my gaze on my feet again.

"I'm giving you a chance to make it right," Hank says. His voice has changed and I have to look at his face to know why. He's got his head tilted like he did in the bookstore when he was listening to Grandpa Henry's voice. His eyes find mine and he smiles again. It's not a good smile, not a kind or happy smile. A crazy smile. "Mother said I should give you a choice. You remember Grandma Josephine, don't you, Lil?"

"I never met her."

Hank's eyebrows scrunch together. "Course you did."

"She died before I was born."

He shoves his hands in his pockets and looks down at the sidewalk. "Can that be right?"

"You're all mixed up. What you did to Mom, it changed you. I think you need to turn yourself in." My words surprise me and I think maybe Margie was right after all about there being strength in me. "If you don't, I'm going to tell Margie you're here."

Hank raises his eyes slowly until he's looking at me again. I can't help but flinch away from him. There's no confusion in his face now. "What did I tell you about that?" he says.

I back slowly away, down the sidewalk, looking around, but there's no one out here and Margie's apartment is too far away for her to hear us. I think about running, but everything inside me feels weak and trembly. A bee is starting up in my ear, promising silence and peace. I try to push it away and think about Binka's whiskers to keep me here.

"I'll make this simple for you, Lily," Hanks says. "Two days. You wrap things up here and then I want you to come back to me." He leans toward me, his finger pointing at my chest. "*You* come back to *me*, got it? You and your mother never should've left in the first place. Only you can make this right now. Understand?"

Nick's Mustang is coming down the block. The last thing I want is for Hank to see him. "Okay," I say quickly. "See you in a couple days then."

Hank stares at me for a few seconds, then backs off toward the black SUV he drove when he worked for Grandpa Henry. The passenger side door where Berkenshire Metalworks used to be is painted over. He gets in and drives off down the road as Nick parks across the street.

"Who was that guy?" Nick says when he steps up on the curb next to me.

"A neighbor."

"He looked pretty pissed off. Was he bugging you?"

I try to control my spinning thoughts. "He thought I had a cat who used his flowerpot as a litter box. I told him Binka doesn't even go outside."

Nick looks down the road where Hank is disappearing around a curve. "What a jerk," he says.

"Yeah, that's one word for him." Everything in me is leaping and thrumming—energy I don't know what to do with. There are no bees right now, just this big something I don't recognize. A ball of energy lighting me up.

"You ready to go?" Nick asks.

I open my mouth to tell him I can't, that I have to stay home now, keep watch, stay tethered, figure out what to do. But then I think about how much I've been doing exactly that, how I've squeezed my life into a tiny box just like Hank did with me and Mom, and I decide I will go with Nick. Hank's coming for me and to keep Margie safe I'm going to have to go with him. One date with Nick. One date and then I'll go. A final good-bye because I know when Hank comes, it won't be for me to go live with him. It will be for me to go die with him.

"I'm ready," I say.

When I get into Nick's car, I'm surprised it looks so new inside. "I thought this was an old car?"

"Yup. Dad and I restored it."

"A Mustang, right?"

Nick nods. "Sixty-four and a half."

"You couldn't spring for a sixty-five?"

He grins, shaking his head. "Don't tell you me don't know the significance of the sixty-four and half Mustang."

"Sorry, useless trivia isn't really my thing," I say.

Nick's mouth pops open and then he's shaking his head in mock horror. "April 17, 1964, the day the Mustang was introduced to the world. At New York's World Fair, since you're asking."

"I don't think I asked. But, wow, that's

fascinating." I'm surprised by the light sarcasm in my voice, this new energy inside my body. I feel relaxed and ready to have my date with Nick. I think maybe it's Hank finally coming along, telling me his plans. Now at least I know what's going to happen and I don't have to try to guess.

Maybe knowing I'm going to die has freed me to live.

Nick looks at me, still shaking his head and grinning. "Sacrilege." He starts the car up, pulls away from the curb and zooms down the road like he's been driving his whole life.

We're quiet for a little while, I think because Nick doesn't know what questions to ask, which ones are safe and which ones would bring on the quiet. It doesn't feel great, being high maintenance, so I get us started.

"Margie found your webpage. At your school?"

Nick nods and his hair dips forward and back. "They made me put that up."

"They're proud of you there."

"I guess."

"So you get to choose what school you go to?"

He glances over at me and is eyebrows are scrunched together in the middle. "Yeah, I guess."

"You don't seem happy about it."

"Have you ever had three people trying to decide your fate, all the choices ones you wouldn't make for yourself?"

"Nope," I say. "I never had three people who cared that much."

Nick looks sorry he complained.

"It's okay. My mom loved me a lot. When I was a kid, Hank did too. It was enough." The words come easier than I expect.

"I'm glad," Nick says. "What was she like, your mom?"

I start to shake my head, ready to tell Nick I

can't talk about Mom yet. But there are words in me to tell about the good times. "She was the best, you know? She always took time to answer my questions, no matter how stupid they were. When I was little I was curious about color, I think because Hank painted." I glance at Nick to make sure he's not falling asleep. He's nodding and I think he gets what I'm saying. "I didn't care about why the sky was blue, though. I wanted to know why blue and red made purple, why yellow and blue made green. This sort of led to a talk about how babies are made. That stopped my questions for awhile."

Nick laughs. "You went from mixing paint colors to making babies in the same conversation?"

"I was a nosy kid, I guess you could say. I had a lot of questions."

"And made some pretty impressive connections."

"I guess. Anyway, Mom turned bright red when I asked how she and Hank got mixed up to make me."

Nick's laughter is all around us in his old-new car. I join him and don't feel even a little like I'm going to rip open.

After a bit we quiet down and I watch the scenery go by outside my window. We're crossing a different bridge this time, heading to a theater Nick says is close to the university.

"So you'll be a junior next year, right?" Nick says.

"Yeah, I guess."

"You guess?"

"I haven't thought much about going back to school."

"What was your last school like?"

The answer to Nick's question bounces around inside me for awhile. It feels like a lifetime ago, my sophomore year. A brand new school. Not one familiar face. Not one friendly one either. Each day a fight to stay invisible, each class torture until the bell rang. The first flutters I ever felt were last year, until the boy I had a crush on announced in English class that, by the smell of me, I was going for the hi-pro glow. I remember a group of girls pinching their noses closed and fake barfing when I walked into the cafeteria, remember eating my lunch in dark corners of empty classrooms after that, remember even the outcasts casting me out.

"It was okay," I finally say.

Nick glances over at me. "You've never had it easy, have you?"

"It's not a right."

"What?"

"To have things easy. It's not a right."

"I know, but it seems like the best people go through the worst kind of hell."

I let his words sink into the hollow place inside me, let them knock around in there like the bees do. With all that Hank said to me over the last two years, all I believed to be true, with my not answering the phone the night he came with his gun, I don't feel like one of the best. But I don't say so. I don't mind Nick thinking I'm good.

We get to the movie theater and Nick has to drive around for a little while before he finds a parking space. We drive past Twice Told Tales where Cheetah-the-cat gave me kisses on my cheek and where Hank sat on the floor with me.

I stay quiet, trying to ignore this new feeling in my stomach, the not-flutters because there's no room. We finally park and Nick tells me to stay where I am. When I see him coming around the car, I understand. He sweeps my door open, holding out a hand. I let him fold my small, cold hand into his big, warm one, let him give me a little tug out of the car. I take mine right back, though, and rub my arms. I feel bare and cold without Mom's sweater even though the night's a warm one.

We walk up the road a little ways to the movie theater. It's a busy night, a lot of kids our age hanging around out front—some smoking, taking drinks from bottles inside paper sacks, talking and laughing in big and small groups.

My stomach sinks, a shiver goes through me and all the new energy in my body leaves as fast as it came along. I pause in front of a little shop just before the theater and pretend to look in the window.

"Are you okay?" Nick asks.

"There are a lot of people here."

"Yes."

I look at Nick, need him to see how turned inside-out I am. He puts his arm around my shoulders. "It's just me and you," he says. His eyes let me know he understands. I let his arm stay so I can absorb some of his strength. His words and his sureness settle into me and I feel better after a bit. We finish our walk and get to the theater, stand in line and wait to buy our tickets. It's not a minute or two before a group of boys starts shoving around behind us. Nick drops his arm from my shoulders when one bumps me hard. He turns around.

"Nicky!" the boy doing most of the shoving says.

"Hey, Bret," Nick says. "Take it easy, huh?"

"Yeah, sorry, man. Didn't see you there." Bret looks me up, down, up, smiling big. "Who's this?"

Nick takes my hand and I hold on tight. "This is Lily. Lily, this is Bret," Nick says and then starts pointing at the other kids in the group. "Paul, Devon, Arturo."

I don't like how they're looking at me—eyes darting from my sneakers to my hair and everywhere in between.

"She's hot, Nicky. Where'd you rustle this one up?" Devon says in a deep, raspy voice, which only deepens my chill.

Nick looks embarrassed and I want to disappear into the sidewalk. My face is burning. Nick's hand over mine, his warmth and the heartbeat I feel in his palm, these are the things I focus on. I think *Nick's heartbeat* and it's enough. For now.

"Hey, see you guys later, okay?" Nick says. He turns, tugs me out of line and back toward his car. "Forgot my wallet, you believe that?"

I glance over my shoulder at the four boys in line. They're all bobbing their heads in unison, hands waving good-bye.

"What are we doing?" I whisper as we walk fast toward Nick's car.

"Sorry," he mutters. He's watching the sidewalk and I think maybe he's embarrassed to be with me. I want to sniff my shirt to see if it's the hi-pro glow boy all over again, but then remember it's a new one. This is a Margie shirt, not a dog food shirt.

We get to Nick's car and he opens the passenger door for me. He hurries to the other side and slips behind the wheel.

"Did I embarrass you?" I say.

He looks at me, his eyes wide. "Of course not."

"Then what's up?"

He leans his forehead against the steering wheel. "I'm sorry," he says again. I don't get the feeling he's saying it to me, though, so I keep quiet.

Nick finally sits up, digs his keys out and starts his car. "There's a park nearby. Would you mind if we went there instead?" He says this without looking at me.

"Sure." I'm only a little worried about Margie getting mad if she finds out.

We're at the park in a few minutes and Nick stops near a big jungle gym. There's an old swing set a little ways away and when we get out of Nick's car, we both head right for it. The swings are those old-timey rubber kind that make your butt mush up around you. They're nice. They face west and all we do for a little while is swing and watch the city lights.

"Are you sure I didn't embarrass you?" I say to Nick.

He shakes his head. "Why would you embarrass me?"

"I don't know. You just wanted out of there so fast."

Nick doesn't say anything at first and then he points to the swing I'm in. "That's where I spaced out after Mom died."

I look around the park with new eyes, imagining Nick here, his mind far away, time passing without him knowing. "Good choice," I say. "It's a pretty park." Except for a clearing where you can see the city lights, the whole place is packed full of trees.

Quiet settles between us while we swing and drag our sneakers in the grooved sand underneath the set. "So… who were those guys?" I finally ask.

Nick glances at me quick, then looks back down at the ground. "Some kids from school."

He doesn't seem like he's going to say anymore, so I ask him another question. "Your friends?"

"No." He looks at me and his eyes are full of hurt. "I used to be a different person, Lily."

"Oh yeah? Are you in witness protection or something? Bet your name's really Hornsby Generica."

A slow grin. "How'd you know?"

"You sort of look like a Hornsby."

"I don't think that's a compliment."

"Probably not."

Nick laughs a little, but the seriousness in him is too big and pretty soon he's frowning again. "Can I tell you something? It's not a good something."

"Sure."

"Those guys in line?"

"Yeah."

"They make up about half the wrestling team at my school."

"Okay."

"And they did used to be my friends."

"Far as I know it's okay to have wrestlers for friends. Nothing in the constitution against it, I don't think."

Nicks smiles again and in his smile is a lot of sadness and regret, I'm pretty sure. "I used to hang out with them because I was afraid they'd target me otherwise."

Something in my stomach knows what Nick's talking about before my head does. It's the same feeling I got around hi-pro glow boy and those girls who would pinch their noses closed when I walked by. "Target you?" I say.

"They're bullies. And I don't mean take-your-lunch-money bullies. I mean corner-you-after-school-and-beat-the-crap-out-of-you bullies."

I stop swinging and stare hard at Nick. "You helped them beat people up?"

"No, but I picked on people. There was one girl in particular. If you wanted to be part of the inner circle, you did what they said. Arturo—the short one?"

Nod.

"He's the one who told me about this girl Georgia. She was big, you know?"

"Yeah, I know." It was the same in the schools I went to—the big girls always got the worst of it.

Nick looks at his feet again. "I teased her." He shakes his head. "Screw that. I tortured her. Day in and day out. You know what it took to make me stop?"

"No."

"She showed up at my door with her mother. The way Georgia's mom explained it, she'd found a suicide note in Georgia's history book and made her say what was going on at school. My parents wanted to kill me. Seriously, I've never been grounded so long before or since."

I don't say anything, instead just wait for Nick to finish. My stomach's settled down, but there's something in me that sees Nick in a different way now. I wish there wasn't.

"Anyway, I stopped hanging out with those guys and apologized to Georgia."

"Is she okay?"

Nick nods. "She's goes to a private school at the other end of town now. I hear she's a lot happier."

"Did the wrestlers start in on you?"

"No and that's kinda the worst thing, you know?"

"You wanted to be punished."

Nick tents his fingers and nods. "Yeah."

"And you didn't want to see the movie even though they don't bug you?"

"The way they looked at you, it reminded me of…"

"Georgia."

Nick shakes his head. "No, not like Georgia. Like the pretty girls they harass."

I think Nick's believing I'm pretty would feel better if I didn't know about Georgia. All I can think is how I like a boy who almost pushed a girl to suicide.

"People change, Lilybeans."

Mom always believed so. It's how she explained Hank going from a real dad who taught me how to ride a bike to a mean dad who said I wasn't good enough. I changed too, the second I saw Mom on the living room floor. I don't remember how I was before, but I know I wasn't empty or hearing bees or seeing not-Hanks. I think I was close to normal, especially when it was just me and Mom. People change. If I changed, if Hank changed, maybe Nick did too.

"I'm glad you don't hurt people anymore," I say. The words sound lame, but they're all I can get out.

"Me too," Nick says. "God, my parents were so disappointed. I never want to see that look in my dad's eyes again."

"Because he knows how it feels."

"Yeah. We all do. Seattle's more open than most places, but people all over have strong opinions."

"I get it," I say.

Nick looks at me from under his long eyelashes. "So do you totally hate me now?"

"Not totally," I say and follow this up with a grin.

Nick swings in close until we're almost nose to nose. "Listen, Spacey, I figure we're even for the dinner party letdown now. Yeah?"

"I guess if you call trading a deep, dark secret for some unrealistic expectations an even swap."

Nick plants a kiss on my cheek, a loud smacker that echoes in the fading light. "Unrealistic my ass."

I can't say anything right now because where Nick kissed me feels like it's lit right up with sparks and tingles. A little circle of life. Nick is good. He did bad things, but now he's good. This is how I will remember this moment.

There's a rumbling across the park. I look up in time to see a black SUV with a painted-over logo on its door disappear around the corner. Maybe Hank's decided I don't get two days after all. I don't know how I thought I could count on him telling me the truth. He'll come—I know this for sure. But even if I choose to go with him, it isn't about living anymore. It's about dying.

Being here with Nick, listening to him talk about the ways he's changed, hearing Margie's words earlier about how she believes I'm strong, I think it's time I make some choices too. I have a lot of stuff to work out and the bees are starting up, letting me know I better get to it.

"I need to go home," I say.

Nick looks at his watch. "It's only been—"

"Nick, please. I need to go home." I get up off the swing and walk fast toward Nick's car. I wait while he opens the door for me.

We're silent all the way to Margie's apartment and Nick looks hurt when I turn to say good night. I lean over and kiss him lightly on the cheek. "I'm sorry," I say. "I'm not feeling very well. Maybe it's a cold or something. You understand?"

"And what? You're giving it to me as a thank you for the park?" He grins, showing me he's glad it's not him I'm upset about.

"It's the least I could do."

I wave at Nick as he pulls away from the curb, then look up and down the street to see if Hank's followed us back. No black SUV, no Hank. I walk fast toward Margie's apartment anyway, trying to outrun the bees.

I almost head on into the quiet place when I'm through the front door, but then Binka scales me, sits on my shoulder and tells me with her nose in my ear how much she missed me when I was out with Nick. She drives the bees away. Margie's curious about why I'm back early, but accepts my words about not feeling up to it after all.

The next morning I decide to look at Dr. Pratchett's workbook to see if it can give me ideas for how to get the bees to disappear. If I can do that, if I can answer their buzzing, maybe I can stay and defend myself against Hank, try to have a new life with Margie, Sam, Nick and Binka.

I grab the workbook out of the canvas bag Dr. Pratchett gave me and set it on the table next to the sun chair, then press down on the binding so it'll stay open on its own. I've put the picture Hank tucked behind the cover at the bottom of a drawer where Margie won't find it.

Binka parks herself in the middle of the first page of my new workbook. She's got her back to me and her head bowed, like she's reading. She twists around to look at me and her ears are all the way forward and I can see she approves, that she thinks it's a good idea I read this book. She wanders off to a fancy pink bed Sam brought over for her and settles in for a long nap.

I read through the introduction and heed the warning about not skipping ahead. Dr. Pratchett wasn't kidding. The book is interesting and I can see why he wants me to go through it. The first thing the book wants me to do is make a list of self-soothing exercises. I like tethers and I like threads and I like bubble baths, so I write these down first. Next the book wants me to try one out. I don't need a tether right now since the bees aren't buzzing and I already have a thread with going through the workbook, so I decide on a bubble bath.

I get the water going, pour in some liquid bubbles Margie's got lying around, then leave to find a towel. I'm fishing one out of the linen closet when the smell of the bubbles hits.

Mom pokes her head around my open bedroom door. "Lilybeans, you're going to spill that water right out of the tub."

"I like it full. I know just when to stop it."

"Okay, kiddo. Don't forget, though."

I wait for a little longer and finally grab up my book and towel and head toward the sound of the whooshing water. A new smell is filling up the bathroom, spilling out into the hall, pushing out the dog food. Vanilla. Lilac. "Did you put something in here?"

"A surprise! For my Lilybeans!"

A surprise because Mom's trying to make up for

Hank. Hank and his anger. Hank and his meanness. Hank and his control. She leaves "happies," she calls them, and she hopes they'll help scrub my memory. She hopes they'll help me know how loved I am.

They do.

My legs go rubbery and I sit down hard in front of the linen closet. The rip that started with Mom's letter explodes into a sob bigger than the world and I feel myself shatter into a million pieces. The sound from me is filling the apartment—my missing Mom flooding every part of me. I feel her fluffy hair on my fingertips and I smell pineapple and I hear the bells as she hangs a wreath on the front door for Christmas and I think about all the movies we watched on the threadbare couch with the pot of gold. I think about the pictures and the hikes and, oh god, all the tears and pain caused by Hank in those last years. The shame, the silence, the ghostly existence we led, the loneliness. And how, through it all, we had each other.

Binka hears me sobbing, comes running, jumps into my arms. She puts her nose under my chin, pressing hard. I hold her because if I don't I'm not going to exist anymore. My tether—Binka. I rock back and forth, the smell of Mom's bubbles taking over everything. All mixed up in me is my stuffed grief for Mom and my terrible guilt for not answering the phone. The buzzing is here and it's so big. So loud. I can answer it or I can go where it's quiet. These are my choices.

I want to go and almost do, but my phone starts playing a tune—the one Margie programmed for Nick's number. It's an old love song she likes, one I don't know. Nick's ring and Binka—my tethers. I don't answer. I listen to the bees and, through them, Nick's song that means he wants to talk to me.

I can go, the buzzing says. I can be quiet, check

out, disappear for awhile. Or forever. I can stop stuffing, let go of all the tethers, the threads, the hollow. Let it all go and float into nothingness.

I take a deep breath. "It's not what I want." My voice in the empty apartment is full of something I don't recognize, something like the energy I felt last night after Hank's visit. I only know it's taken a lot for me to say these words, to say there's something I don't want. Because not wanting something means the opposite is true too.

I want to live.

First, I make myself stand. Then I take one step. Another. Three steps, another. Binka trots after me, not interested in being on my shoulder when I'm going toward running water. The tub is full almost to the top. I shut the water off and pull the plug out. If I'm going to answer the buzzing, the ringing, I better not be up to my neck in water.

My phone isn't playing a tune anymore when I get back to my bedroom. It's quiet on my nightstand. I pick it up and find where Margie's programmed Dr. Pratchett's number. He said to call if I need him. If he has a patient, I'll have to wait. If he's busy, I'll feel stupid.

"Call me anytime, Lily. If I don't answer, leave a message and I'll get back to you as soon as I can."

I push the button that will make my phone call Dr. Pratchett. It's on the fifth ring and I think he's not going to answer when he does. "Dr. Pratchett speaking."

"Hi, Dr. Pratchett, this is Lily… Berkenshire?" My voice, shaky. My soul, here.

"Lily! It's good to hear from you. How are you?"

"I'm ready to answer the buzzing, but it feels like it has to be today. Now." I wonder if he'll remember us talking about the bees.

He's silent for a moment, then says, "Okay, Lily. Wait just a moment?"

"Okay."

I hear Dr. Pratchett put down his phone and shuffle around in his office. Pretty soon his soft voice is there again, only far away, not talking to me. I hear, "Have the afternoon open."

"Bring her now?"

"I'll tell her."

"Lily?" Dr. Pratchett says in my ear. "Are you there?"

"I'm here."

"Margie can't get away from work right now, but she's sending Sam to pick you up. He'll bring you here. Okay?"

"Okay."

"I'll see you in a little while."

We hang up. I get dressed, tell the bees to knock it off already and pull a brush through my hair. Sam's here faster than I expect. I shove my feet into shoes, kiss Binka good-bye and lock up the apartment.

Sam drops me off in front of Dr. Pratchett's big glass building and gives me a loud smack on the cheek. "Go kick some bee ass, Lilykins."

I grin at Sam and hope I can. For now, the bees are a whisper in the background, waiting and not waiting.

Dr. Pratchett's inside the big glass doors. We ride up in the elevator together and head right into his office. I decide maybe answering the bees will be easier if I don't sit in my normal chair. I decide on the couch instead and sink down into leather smooshiness. That Christmas smell is all around me. I don't feel like a cliché after all.

"I hope you didn't kick anyone out for me," I say, worried now that I took another crazy's time-slot.

"My afternoon is free," Dr. Pratchett says. He smiles his warm smile.

"Thanks for seeing me."

He nods, says in a cautious voice, "So, Margie told me about your spell on the bus after you left here last week. Would you like to talk a little about that before we get to the bees?"

"Didn't Margie tell you already?"

"Yes, but I'd like to hear your version. And I think it will help us understand more about the bees."

"I checked out for awhile. Then I woke up. Then I went home to Margie's apartment." I don't tell Dr. Pratchett about Hank's picture. Not yet. I think it's important I answer the buzzing first.

"Does it scare you to be so vulnerable?"

I look down at my lap, at my clasped hands. I think about Hank and his promise to come for me tomorrow. "No room for fear," I say, but I already know it's not true anymore. Now there's Binka, Margie, Sam, Nick. Now there are people and a life I don't know if I can fit into, but one I don't feel much like leaving. There's stuff.

"Still hollow?" Dr. Pratchett asks.

"Yes."

"Something Margie said tells me a different story."

I look up, trying to guess what Dr. Pratchett's talking about. Maybe he sees I'm not sure about there being no room for fear. "What do you mean?"

"She said you comforted her. You held her when she was afraid."

"My spell on the bus wasn't her fault."

"No, of course not. But she thought it was."

"Yes." I'm so confused my head is spinning.

"Lily, when a person is truly hollowed out, when someone has no room in here"—Dr. Pratchett pats his chest where his heart is—"when you don't feel anything for yourself—like fear—you don't feel things for other people."

"Okay."

"You felt empathy for Margie."

"Empathy's easy."

Dr. Pratchett smiles. "Not for everyone. Do you know, not everyone would have taken Binka out of that dumpster? Many people would have just walked right by."

"I know. We're separate. Disconnected."

"Tell me what you mean."

"Everything's filtered through something. Phones. Doors. Cameras. People feel separate, so they don't help."

Dr. Pratchett's nodding. "Do you think that's why someone else would have left Binka?"

Nod.

"And yet you jumped in. Margie said you didn't hesitate for a second."

"No."

"Lily, someone who doesn't have room inside for feelings doesn't do these things. Someone who sees the separation you were just talking about can't *not* feel. You see things many people never do." Nick's words in Dr. Prachett's throat.

"Okay."

"Do you remember our first visit, when you told me you didn't have room for anything but emptiness? No room for love or happiness or anything but that sense of being tin?"

"Yes."

"I believe you have room for it all."

I watch Dr. Pratchett for a little while. I get what he's saying. "Maybe, if I make room, if I answer the buzzing, I might not have any more spells?"

"Yes."

"Can you help me?"

"I hope so. Let's start with what you believe the buzzing represents."

"I said already."

"Yes, the phone in your old house." Dr. Pratchett pauses and shifts in his scrunchy leather chair. "The bees precede a dissociative spell."

"Yes."

"The pattern is like a ringing telephone."

"Yes."

"Your father used to call you on the phone when he was drunk."

"Yes."

"What would he say?"

"Did you know she's hiding money? Did you know she's sleeping with every guy she meets? Did you know you're poor for no reason? For nothing? Lily?"

I shake my head, not ready to say the words out loud, deciding I need to ask Dr. Pratchett a question about Mom first. I couldn't hear it in our last session, but I think I can now. "Could you tell me first what Hank said to my mom when he would call her at work?"

Dr. Pratchett looks unsure, then leans forward. "Apparently he wanted you both back home. He made promises your mother didn't believe."

"Promises?"

"He said he would stop working for his father if the two of you rejoined him."

"And she didn't believe him?"

"No."

"Why?"

"Because when she suggested he stop working for his father first and they move slowly toward reconciliation, he became enraged."

"He told her she had no right to call the shots, to say what we would do."

Dr. Pratchett's quiet for a minute, then leans back in his chair. "That's right, Lily."

"It's the same thing he said when we were at home. Mom was right not to believe him."

"So it would appear. Would you like to discuss

what Hank said to you on the phone now?"

I look around the room, at the books on Dr. Pratchett's shelves, smell the spicy and the leather. I feel safe. I can say the words here, let some of it out. "He said, 'Did you know she's hiding money? Did you know she's sleeping with every guy she meets? Did you know you're poor for no reason? For nothing? Lily?'" The words are like a chant in my head, a terrible poem that won't let go.

"How did Hank's words make you feel?"

I take a breath and grab a tissue out of the box on the coffee table in front of me. "I hated when he said those things, but they also made me doubt, you know?"

"You wondered if the words were true."

"Yeah, even though deep down I knew they weren't."

"Did your father say similar things about you?"

"Different. That I was stupid mostly."

"Just in those last years or always?"

I think about Hank before he started working for Grandpa Henry. "Mostly in those last years, but sometimes before."

"When he'd been drinking?"

"Yes." I look at the clock on Dr. Pratchett's desk. "Am I making you late?"

He doesn't look at the clock, keeps focused on me. "No, Lily. We're fine. I have the whole afternoon, remember?"

I feel confused. All this talking, all this answering the bees. It's a lot.

Dr. Pratchett breathes and I breathe and pretty soon he asks another question. "Can you tell me what prompted you to answer the buzzing now?"

"I started the workbook and made a list of my soothing thingies?"

"Yes."

"One was a bubble bath. Margie has the same

bubbles Mom gave me."

"I see. So the smell triggered the bees?"

"Yes."

"Did you dissociate?"

"No. I decided not to."

Dr. Pratchett's quiet, working something out. "Lily, do you trust me?"

I don't even have to think. "Yes."

"What I'm going to ask you to do will be difficult, but I believe you're ready. You stopped a dissociative spell, which tells me you're beginning to accept what happened. You understand?"

"I have more control now."

"Exactly. Here's what I'd like you to do. I want you to pretend Hank is sitting in that empty chair over there." Dr. Pratchett's pointing to the chair I sat in during my other sessions, the one I chose because I didn't want to be a cliché. "Think you can do that?"

I think I can do that because already I'm smelling whiskey, even a little mint, definitely paint mixed in with the Christmas spice. Pretty soon not-Hank is sitting in the empty chair, his hands resting on his knees, his dull eyes watching me.

"I can do that," I say.

"Good." Dr. Pratchett pauses, breathes, says, "I'd like you to talk about how you were affected the night your mother died. Say it like you're telling Hank."

I suck in my breath. Can I speak these words? The words that say what happened? A few bees start knocking around in my head, buzzing their promise song. It's the quiet place or it's answer them. Dr. Pratchett's watching me closely, his afternoon for me because I want to answer the bees. It's time to say the words. Out loud. I stop thinking, start talking. Not to Dr. Pratchett, but to not-Hank.

"When you came that night with your gun, when you killed my mother." I tap my chest, showing not-Hank where he made me hollow. "I disappeared that day. You changed me. I don't remember how I was before. I only know there was more and that you made me hollow. You emptied me out with your bullets, with your killing Mom. When you took her, you took me."

Not-Hank's whispered words coil around me, in me, try to bring on the bees.

"Your fault, Beans. You should have answered the phone."

"You're too stupid to do that."

"You don't call the shots, little girl."

"Sometimes I wonder if she's really my daughter."

"Two peas in a pod, you and your mother. Stupid, lazy, useless."

"Did you know she's hiding money? Did you know she's sleeping with every guy she meets? Did you know you're poor for no reason? For nothing? Lily?"

"One year into two. Two years into nothing."

"You're the only one who can make this right now, Beans."

I push his words past me, don't let them sink in. I think I understand. The ringing, the buzzing, it's the lies he told, all the things he tried to make me believe—about myself, about Mom. It's his drunk voice and his anger and his belief that he knew what was best for us. It's Mom's voice too, trying to undo the damage. It's her happies and the year we were alone together, making a new life. It's everything. My whole life right there in the ringing of a telephone.

And the hollow. I get it now. This empty space inside me can get filled up with acceptance and moving forward, like Margie, or it can get filled up with rage and craziness, like Hank. It's my choice what I fill it with. Looking at not-Hank, I know it would be easy to let the insanity in, to let my heart shrivel for good. That way, there's no pain. Just rage. Or quiet.

The knocking-around bees start buzzing louder. The quiet place is tugging even though I'm answering. It's on the other side of this breath—a promise of forever peace. So what if he lied? I believed him even though I knew. He was my father, the man who said he loved me, the man who taught me about how much people can hurt other people. Maybe it's easier just to go, to fade away into quiet, peace, to dissolve and become a speck in a world full of specks.

Margie's face is in my mind. Her smiling, sparkling eyes as she hands me the tin box she made cry.

"Tin isn't very interesting just flat. It's got a lot more character when it's been stressed and molded. The only way to do that is to bend it until it cries."

I lean forward and wrap my arms around my legs. I feel myself bending, crying, answering.

"Are you okay, Lily?" Dr. Pratchett asks. His voice is quiet, but not far away. That's when I realize I'm not hearing him through the buzzing because the buzzing's gone.

"I'm okay," I say. I sit up slowly and look at the empty chair where not-Hank was. He's over by the bookcase now and he's changing. First to a shiny metal like the small box Margie said is the toughest of the bunch, then to dull silver like the tin box Margie had to bend to make beautiful, then to copper and silver, then layered shale like the delicate box that looks strong but isn't. He's flaking apart little by little, breaking into a million pieces. Pretty soon he's gone and he takes his whiskey, paint and mint with him.

I only smell Christmas.

Dr. Pratchett comes over and sits next to me.

"How do you feel, Lily?"

"I guess maybe I feel better." It's true. Maybe not all the way better, but enough better to make the bees go, to make not-Hank go. "I think the buzzing was Hank's lies about me and my mom. I believed him because he taught me how to ride a bike, how to read, how to paint a picture."

"He was your dad," Dr. Pratchett says softly.

"Yeah." My voice hitches and pretty soon I'm using that tissue again, only my crying isn't for Mom this time. "I loved him. I always thought he loved me. Even when he was mean, I thought he did."

"Do you think it's possible he both loved you and felt compelled to control you?"

"Be over in just a minute, sweetheart."

"I love you, Beans. We'll all be together now. Hold real still, honey."

"See you later."

"I think he believed we would better off not here anymore, that we would be together again after he shot me. Shot himself." Dr. Pratchett is quiet and it takes me a little bit to realize my mistake. He touches my arm, asks me with his fingertips to look at him.

"Lily, you told Margie your father didn't try to hurt you that night." His voice is cautious, full of questions.

My stomach is all flutters and nervous energy. "I lied, Dr. Pratchett. Hank tried to kill me too. He was out of bullets by the time he was close enough."

Silence, then more caution. "Did he say anything that would indicate he would come back for you?"

I decide I don't want to lie anymore. No more lying, no more stuffing. Even if it means Mack and Darcy. I nod and see something in Dr. Pratchett's eyes I haven't before. Fear. "Have you seen him,

Lily? In Seattle?"

"Yes," I say. "In the bookstore. And he was on the bus with me during my spell. He left me a picture of me and Margie in Mom's meadow. Then last night he came to Margie's apartment when I was waiting outside for Nick." Dr. Pratchett looks confused. "Nick is my friend—we went on a date. Hank was there before he picked me up. He said I have to make things right, that he wants me to live with him again, but I have to choose to come back. I think he's been other places too, but sometimes I wasn't sure if he was real." I don't know if it's the time to tell Dr. Pratchett about the not-Hanks, about how his whiskey and mint smell meant that he wasn't really there.

Dr. Pratchett looks like he wants to ask, but decides to focus on real-Hank instead. "The bookstore—is this when you went with Margie before our first visit?"

"Yes, when I met Cheetah."

"What did he say to you, Lily?" Dr. Pratchett's voice is still careful, like he's afraid I'm going to stop talking. I'm not going to stop. I'm ready to not be hollow anymore.

"He said it wasn't time yet, that when it was, we would go to Grandpa Henry's."

"And did you hear anything Hank said to you on the bus?"

"No. He just left me that picture."

Dr. Pratchett nods, his eyes all worry. "And you didn't see him again until last night?"

"He was maybe at Pike's Place when I went there with Nick."

"And you haven't told Margie?"

I shake my head, ashamed. "I was afraid she would send me away. To Mack and Darcy's?"

"I don't know who Mack and Darcy are," Dr. Pratchett says.

I'm surprised. I thought Margie would talk to Dr. Pratchett about Mack and Darcy's ranch, but she hasn't. "Didn't Margie want to send me away?"

Dr. Pratchett shakes his head. "Never."

I'm looking at Dr. Pratchett and I can feel my eyes are big, that I've got my deep pools going. I'm so surprised Margie never want to send me away I don't know what to say. I keep quiet, though, and let the new feeling inside me spread.

The hollow place was so heavy before. This new feeling is light. I think Dr. Pratchett was right—there's room inside for everything. Mom's face, her smile, they're right there in my mind and I imagine her here, grinning at me, telling me she's proud I stopped stuffing. Imagining Mom makes the tears start up again, but they don't make me rip, don't dissolve me. I think they're something like normal tears, the ones you cry when someone you love isn't here anymore.

Dr. Pratchett reaches over and pats my arm. "Are you okay?"

"I'm okay," I say. For the first time I mean it.

"That was quite a breakthrough, Lily, and I want to thank you for trusting me." He smiles and points to the phone on his desk. "I'm going to need to call Margie now. You understand?"

"Tell her Hank's in town."

"Yes."

"Tell her I'm sorry, too?"

Dr. Pratchett smiles and heads on over to his desk. He's talking to Margie and I'm walking around his office now, touching his books again. I run my fingers down the spine of *The Stand* and think about how Stu Redman didn't get to make his final stand against the Dark Man. He broke his leg along the way and had to stay behind. The plan for Stu was bigger than facing the Dark Man. He didn't know it was bigger, though, didn't even know how he was going to fit or where he belonged. But he trusted.

I decide to be like Stu, to trust that I'll fit into this new life.

I decide to trust that there's a plan for me.

PART III

She was no longer wrestling with the grief,
but could sit down with it as a lasting companion
and make it a sharer in her thoughts.
-George Eliot, *Middlemarch*

While Margie's rushing to Dr. Pratchett's office from her work, I'm talking with Nick on the phone, asking him if he wants to say good-bye before we leave. Margie's decided we're not staying in Seattle, that we'll borrow Sam's cabin on San Juan Island until Officer Archie and his friends in Washington can catch Hank. Sam will take Binka and keep her safe.

Nick's at Pike's Place and will have to run back to meet me in front of the dancing fountains. It's why he was calling earlier, to see if I wanted to go with, if I was still in the market for a personal fish, a panama hat, maybe some more daisies. I think now if I heard the old guy with a lot of hope singing about shouting down the wind, I might think different. I might have something more to say about that.

Dr. Pratchett takes me downstairs and stands

with me in the lobby until we see Nick running up the wide concrete stairs.

"I'll stay here until Margie picks you up," he says.

"Thanks, Dr. Pratchett." I head on out to the fountains, giving Nick a little wave. He trots over, grins, gives me a big hug without asking. I don't mind the not asking. Don't mind at all.

I keep quiet about answering the buzzing, not sure if Nick would understand. This is good-bye for a little while and I don't want there to be a bunch of weird words between us. We're only starting out, me and Nick.

"I wish you didn't have to leave," Nick says. He still hasn't pulled his arms away. I listen to his heartbeat, quick and strong. My body feels his heat. Where he touches is alive, and where he doesn't is alive too.

"I wish that too," I say. "I'll miss you." The words are easy. So easy.

Nick pulls back, his face surprised. "Don't tease me, Berkenshire."

"I'm not, Hornsby."

Nick's smile makes me smile and pretty soon we're grinning at each other like it's the best day of our lives. Full goof.

"You seem different," Nick says.

"I am different." Nick doesn't know how I was before Hank came with his gun. I don't remember, but I do know he's right—I am different.

"So, you going to change your name?" Nick says.

"Henrietta Livingstock," I say right away.

Nick laughs, shaking his head. "Please, god, no, anything but Henrietta."

"What's wrong with Henrietta?"

Nick just shakes his head again, then fishes around in his pocket and pulls something out. "I bought you this," he says. "Down at Pike's." He holds it up in the bright day so I can see. It's a necklace on a thin, silver chain. My breath catches and I can't joke anymore, can't believe Nick bought me this necklace.

"It's stained glass," he's saying. "The guy I bought it from said the glass and metal were forged together." He points to the dull silver holding the tiny pieces of colored glass together. "There's no glue. Just metal and glass. I guess it's unique or something."

I take the necklace from Nick, slip it over my head and study the fragments of glass—once shattered grains, barely sticking, now whole.

"It's perfect."

"Didn't mean to make you cry, Henrietta." Nick brushes my cheek with his thumb.

"Someday I'm going to tell you how important this necklace is." I smile at him, then slip my arms around his neck. "Thank you."

Nick pulls back from our hug, but doesn't let me go. He leans in, his eyes slipping slowly closed. When his lips kiss mine, they are soft and warm. His hands move behind me and I feel his fingers just barely touching my back. Ten spots of pure softness. Ten spots that tell me he knows what I need, what I can handle. I let Nick kiss me and I kiss him back. I move my hands up his arms, feel him shiver, press my palm against his cheek. In this moment Nick's lips, his hands, they're all I want. I don't care if the wind's kicking up and sending spray from the fountains to coat our skin. I don't care that we're right out in public where anyone can see us. I don't care that my phone is playing a tune.

Nick does, though. He breaks our kiss and points at my pocket. "Margie'll kill me for keeping you like this."

"Hi, Aunt Margie," I say after I peek at the caller ID.

"Hey, kiddo. Sorry to interrupt, but we've gotta hit the road." I'm relieved Margie doesn't sound mad.

"Where are you?"

Instead of Margie's answer, I hear her honk. She's where the bus picks people up and drops them off. She waves. I wave back, then turn to Nick. "I'll call you as soon as I can, okay?"

He's serious now. "Be careful, okay?"

"I'll be careful." I give Nick another quick hug, whisper good-bye and trot toward Margie's car. I remember to wave to Dr. Pratchett still inside the big glass doors before I get too far. He waves back.

"See ya, Henri!" Nick calls out as I'm opening Margie's car door.

"See ya, Hornsby!" I holler right back. My voice cracks a little because I haven't done much yelling lately, not even much talking if we're being honest. It's good, though. My voice cracking means I'm alive.

We go back to the apartment so we can pick up our clothes, some books, a couple of Margie's boxes, her laptop. I'll have to say good-bye to Binka, try to explain to her about Sam and his two cats. I'll tell her to be brave meeting them and ask her to not teach them any of her bad manners and spazzy ways unless she needs to. I think if I get Binka back after Hank's caught, I'll be lucky. Sam loves her.

Sam's waiting outside the apartment when we get there, his hair going twenty different ways as usual. "Kick some bee ass, Lilykins?"

"Damn straight," I say.

He grins and gives me a squeeze while Margie unlocks the door.

I expect to see Binka sitting in the entryway or the living room like usual, waiting to pounce the second we get in. But she's nowhere. This makes my legs go weak even before I hear Margie's holler and Sam's gasp. They're looking at something over by my favorite chair next to the patio, something I don't care about right now because I have to find Binka. I run to my bedroom, call her name, then when she doesn't come, scream her name. I drop to my knees and look under my bed. She's there, tucked into a corner, her spaz fur sticking out even more than usual, her eyes huge and terrified.

It takes a minute to coax her out and then her body stays rigid when I hold her against my cheek. Even before I go back into the living room I know why Binka's so scared. Hank's been here.

Sure enough, Margie and Sam are over by the sun chair, their shoulders bent while they look at something.

"Oh my god," Margie says.

In my chair is a new painting. It's just me in Mom's meadow this time, my cheek resting on my bent arm, my eyes closed, paint splatters running up the page like blood. My skin is two-toned, like Hank understands that he made me into someone else when he killed Mom. Flowers bloom up around me—the Susans and the honeysuckle and the dogwood, the bluebells. I take a step closer. Something catches the light, something not in the picture. There's gold dust on the flowers, in the air around me. He painted Mom's ashes gold. It is the most beautiful painting I have ever seen. Beautiful and terrible.

On the table next to the sun chair is a collage. Me and Margie stepping into the bus the first day we visited Dr. Pratchett's building. Me and Hank at the bookstore, Cheetah in my lap. Margie wearing goggles and an apron, bending over a liquid fire, her gloved hand pointing to something. Binka in the dumpster on her coffee can, her pink mouth open wide, meowing her head off. Me and Nick on the bench at Pike's Place, the water stretching out golden in front of us.

I get closer to the paintings. They're amazing in a way I've never seen before. Hank's art was always just average, never good enough for a gallery or even to get A's in his classes at college. I found a painting once with an evaluation clipped to it. His professor said he needed to dig deeper, that his technique was perfect, but there was no feeling in his work. Looking at Hank's new paintings, I think his professor would say different now. Hank's gone all the way crazy and found the feeling he needs to be a good painter. A great painter.

Binka follows me back to the closet where Margie's stored the big box of pictures, paintings and sculptures from the dog food house. I haven't looked in the box since we came to Seattle, couldn't handle seeing Mom's pictures, her love. But now I pull out two of Hank's paintings, the one where he sliced my cheeks, another from when I was younger. I set them up next to the new paintings. Compared to the meadow, Margie and her liquid fire, me and Nick on the bench, Hank's old stuff looks like it was painted by someone just starting out.

I'm looking at the meadow painting, trying to figure Hank out when I hear Margie dialing her phone. She's talking to a detective, telling him Hank's been in the apartment. After she hangs up she says we have to go. Fast.

Margie disappears into where our bedrooms are, then comes back into the living room a few minutes later, a suitcase that has clothes sticking out of it in one hand, her laptop in the other. "I grabbed some of your things too, Lily. We'll buy whatever else we need."

Margie puts the suitcase by the front door and starts digging in her purse.

"Aunt Margie?" She looks at me and I see her eyes are frantic, scared. "I'm sorry I didn't tell you about Hank being here."

She nods and starts digging again. "We need to go, Lily."

I cross the room and take one of Margie's little heavy boxes down from a bookshelf so I can have a touchstone, turn it around and around in my hands, feel its weight in my palm. There's no lid on this one, just a solid box of pretty silver, perfectly square, etched with symbols I don't recognize. One looks like a house, one a backward five, one a fence with a bird on it. I know my mind is making pictures of these characters, that it's really a different language. Chinese, I think.

"Know what that means?" Sam asks.

"Does it mean 'strong box that looks weak' ?"

He grins and brushes one finger over the letters. "It means *Always Remember*."

"That's in Margie's photo album, too."

Sam nods and glances at Margie where she's standing near the entryway. She comes over to the bookcase where Sam and I are studying her Always Remember box. "The only way I could let go of my father's cruelty was to always remember what he did to us."

Now that I've answered the bees, I understand Margie's words. "If we forget, we might do the same things," I say. "If we remember, we can work hard to be something different."

Margie nods and wraps her arms around me. I wrap mine around her and lay my head on her shoulder. "I love you, Aunt Margie."

She goes tense, then pulls me tighter. "I love you too, Lilybeans."

We leave the apartment after our big hug is

finished, take Margie's bulging suitcase, her laptop, the silver box that means Always Remember. Sam takes Binka in her carrier and promises to spoil her rotten so when we get her back she's an even bigger monster. It's hard saying good-bye to Binka.

Sam waits for us to get to Margie's car, then waves when I wave, smiles when I smile. His eyes are lit up like usual, but worried too. I wish I'd told Margie about Hank being in Seattle now. My silence has made it so Hank could hunt me, hunt us all.

"We cannot control the choices other people make." Dr. Pratchett's words in my head, reminding me that Hank's the one who came with his gun and made his choice that changed me into a quiet girl.

Hank drives up while Margie's getting the bulging suitcase into the trunk.

The whole world slows down and I see things I didn't when Hank was here before. His license plates have been switched from Utah to Washington and the paint he used to cover up the Berkenshire Metalworks logo is flaking off, like he used the wrong kind. He stops the big SUV so he's blocking Sam from seeing us and blocking us from leaving. Margie doesn't notice him right away. He jumps out, all spindly legs and arms, a gun raised at Margie. A bigger one with more bullets.

It's like I'm back in the dog food house, going down the stairs, trying to figure out all the quiet. The whole world is moving through molasses, but I'm not. I shove Margie out of the way and stand in front of Hank's gun. He tries to get around me, but Margie's on the ground and I'm in his face.

"Don't you touch her," I say.

Hank looks from Margie to me, back to Margie. Back to me. "What do you think you're doing, Beans?"

"I'm leaving with my aunt. I don't want to go with you."

Hank's whole body twitches and now he moves his gun to point at my head. "What did I tell you?"

"That I had a choice. I'm not choosing you."

This makes Hank hesitate for a second. "What makes you think you have a choice?"

"You said I had to choose to come back to you. I choose not to."

Hank's breathing fast, hard and his cheeks are reddening past the usual alcoholic blush. My stomach is turning and turning and my hands are shaking and my eyes, I'm pretty sure my eyes can't get any bigger. I hold Hank's attention, make him watch me. It's easy to see he's been drinking. His gun slowly sinks until it's pointing at the road.

I hear a car door slam and raise one hand to stop Sam as he comes around the front of Hank's SUV. He stops, but Hank's seen him. He turns, raises his gun again, points it at where Sam's frozen.

"Go!" I holler as loud as I can. Sam doesn't move. "Go!" My voice echoes off the cars around us.

"Lily..." Sam says in a small voice.

"Sam, get out of here now." I don't holler this time, just say the words so he knows he has to go. Finally, he does.

"Don't you touch her, Hank," Margie says. Her voice cracks on her brother's name. Her brother who she loved once, maybe still does.

"I'll do what I want with her, Marjorie. She's *my* daughter."

Hank's words make Margie take a step toward him. He's raising the gun again when I smack him across the face. "I will not go with you if you hurt my aunt," I say. "You'll have to kill us here and that won't free you of *him* will it?"

Hank's face gets redder, his eyes get wider, his hands start to shake. Pretty soon he's got his arm around me, but not like at the dog food house, not like when I was a kid and he was giving me a hug after I fell off my bike, not like he's ever loved me. He wraps his arm around my neck, points the gun at my head and drags me backward until we're at the open door of Grandpa Henry's SUV.

"Don't worry, Aunt Margie," I say before he shoves me inside and follows.

Margie runs to his door and I try to open mine, but he's locked us in.

"Child-proofed. If only everything were that easy," Hank says. He raises the gun and hits me hard on the head. I want to yell from the pain, but darkness comes before I can.

I wake up a little at a time and keep my body still so Hank won't know. I'm slumped against the passenger door, my forehead on the cool glass. My seatbelt's on and my wrists are taped together. He's humming to himself, driving fast down a straight road.

I look out the window without moving my head. It's nighttime. I've been out for hours. We could be anywhere. All I can see is the outline of a forest—not individual trees because it's too dark, but a jagged wall, a dark shadow against light from stars, from the moon. Every part of me hurts. It's agony to stay still.

Hanks stops humming, leans over and tangles his fist in my hair, yanking me upright. "Don't pretend you're still out."

If staying still was painful, having my hair and

body wrenched is pure agony. I press my lips together to keep my scream inside. When I see Hank wipe his hand off on his jeans, I realize my head is wet and sticky, my hair matted.

"Where are we?"

Hank backhands me in the mouth. Not hard enough to knock my teeth out, but hard enough. I hit the headrest, rebound back and feel a little blood trickle from my cut lip.

"You don't ask any questions. You sit there, quiet."

Hank's never hit me before. He came close once when I spilled my coke on his barcalounger, raised his hand, pulled it back, but ended up yelling at me instead, said I was clumsy, stupid, lazy. His smacks hurt a lot and my head throbs when I twist my neck to see out his window. More forest on that side too.

Hank's wrapped the tape so tight around my wrists my fingers are ten fat sausages. I wiggle them, trying to get some feeling back.

He drives, listening to his music and tapping his fingers against the steering wheel. This is a new Hank, much crazier than the one who came for Mom. I think this Hank is all the way gone, no trace of Dad. Even his face looks different, twisted up with rage and crazy. I keep quiet, hoping I don't get hit again. Not sure if my head could take another smack. I'm a little dizzy, out of it. Not in a bees sort of way, but a being knocked upside the head with a gun sort of way.

The whole front seat of Grandpa Henry's SUV smells like whiskey. One of Hank's huge bottles is jammed between his legs, another full one on the seat between us. He uncaps the already open one with painted fingers, takes a drink, swerves a little while he does.

I'm trying to breathe, trying to figure out how

Hank went from being my dad to being this crazy when he puts the cap back on his whiskey bottle and drums it with a happy little flourish. He throws back his head, laughs, then turns to me. He's grinning in a way that, in the dim dashboard lights, makes him look strangely regretful. For just a second I see the man who used to be my dad, the person who hated his jobs but went anyway because we needed money. Then he grins even bigger and he's Hank again with Grandpa Henry in his head. "Know what I decided while you were at Margie's?"

The way Hank's looking at me now, with his maniacal grin, his glowing eyes, his happy, lifted expression, I decide I don't care why he's gone crazy, only that he has. I shake my head a little. He laughs—a long series of whooping giggles that makes me shrink against the door.

"I decided you don't get to have nice things when you don't do what you're told." Hank winks at me. "I made it quick, though. Margie and her boyfriend." He makes a gun with his fingers. "Bang. Bang. Dead."

I stop moving all at once. Everything in me gives way. My whole body sinks. Sam had gone back to his car when Hank knocked me out. Hadn't he? Marge was okay, but she was trying to get into Hank's SUV I think. Everything's so murky, like trying to find my memories through a thick fog.

I'm back at the dog food house, hearing the loud crack I thought was my song getting played too many times, smelling the thick fog of gunpowder in the living room, my nose denying everything until I saw Mom dead on the floor, seeing Hank laughing, him chasing me in his drunk, clumsy way, feeling the emptiness come on in those moments when the truth of it all finally sank in. Hank killed someone he once loved. A sister who left him and a guy he doesn't know are nothing to him.

But Hank's a liar, a crazy liar who would say anything to make this worse. "I don't believe your lies anymore, Hank." I say these words in a voice loud enough for him to hear and understand.

"Don't you dare call me by my given name."

"I can't call you Dad anymore. My dad's gone." Hank looks at me, his face twisted into something like disbelief and rage.

"Why did you kill my mother?" I say.

He slams his fist down on my thigh. It hurts so much I have to straighten my leg until the muscles stop spasming.

"You don't get to ask the questions."

"Why are you like this?" The words slip out and I can't pull them back in.

Before Hank can answer or hit me again, my cell phone starts making a ruckus on the seat between us. Hank grabs it and flips it open with one hand.

"Lilybean's phone. How may I be of service?" His voice, high-pitched sarcasm.

I hear Margie screaming at the top of her lungs on the other end of my phone and my whole body breathes out. Alive. Margie's alive. Sam too, I just know it. "If you hurt her, Hank, I'll kill you myself!"

Hank twists around so he's looking at me. He smiles and winks. Margie keeps screaming. I can see he's been torturing her for awhile now, probably telling her I'm dead, me not being able to tell her different. I know if I say anything Hank will hit me again. Maybe worse this time. Doesn't matter. Margie needs to know I'm alive. I wait for a quiet space, then yell as loud as I can. "I'm okay, Aunt Margie!"

Hank smacks my leg with the cell phone, then holds it to his ear again. "If she does that again, she won't be for long," he says to Margie while he looks at me.

There's screaming again, but I can't make out the words. Hank waits until it's quiet. "Really, Marjorie. Do you think that's helping your niece?"

More screaming. I smile a little at my strong Aunt Margie. If anyone will find me, it's her. She won't give up. I send out hope, a wish that Hank won't turn off the cell phone. He's never been much on technology, but he watches a lot of TV—those detective shows that say you can be tracked by a cell signal.

Hank snaps the phone closed mid-holler, Margie's voice cut off so fast the silence left behind makes me dizzier. He sets it down on the seat between us again and wags a finger at me while he smiles. "Don't even think about it, Beans."

"You lied about Margie and Sam. You didn't hurt them."

"You don't quiet down, I'll turn around right now and kill them all, including that cute little kitten of yours. It'd be your fault, too."

My fault. I think about the phone ringing that night, me not answering. "If I'd picked up the phone none of this would be happening," I say. I don't think I believe this anymore, but the little bit of hollow left in me wouldn't mind knowing for sure.

Hank lifts a hand and I flinch. He lets it hang in the air for a few seconds—a threat while I cower against the door—and finally lowers it slowly back to the steering wheel. "I don't know what the hell you're talking about." His voice is all twisted in on itself. Angry doesn't even touch where he's coming from now. His hands clench the steering wheel tight and his face, cast green by the instrument panel, is wrinkly with rage.

I smash myself harder against the door, trying to

get as far from him as I can. "When you called that night, I should have answered. I should have listened to you about Mom."

Hank glances at me, his eyes squinty. "My father was right the whole time." He shakes his head and turns back to the road. "I'm surrounded by idiots."

Something in me is all fluttery, alive, demanding answers. "Did you call that night?"

"Why would I call you?" he rages. "I was coming over!" Hank's shaking his head again, this time with his mouth pursed like he's tasting something sour. "Soon as I got my hands on Dad's will, I went over. You two sure weren't coming back if there wasn't any money, huh, Beans?"

I can't speak, can't think about Hank's crazy reasoning. I look from the passing trees to his dark profile. "We loved you," I say. I know he'll hit me for it and he does, but it's not as hard.

"You left me," Hank says. "Alone. With him. And then you didn't come back."

I remind Hank of his words. "You said he was right."

Hank doesn't like the tone of my voice and lets me know with the back of his hand again. This one barely hurts.

"You were my dad," I say because the words won't stay inside anymore. "You loved us once, wanted to protect us from Grandpa Henry. You chose us."

I'm crying now, the tears slipping down my face, into an open cut on my cheek, making it sting. "I loved it when you painted me."

Hank shakes his head, his mouth frowning.

"I used to complain, but I loved it. The one you cut up was my favorite until the one of me in the meadow. You're a better painter now." I'm talking mostly to myself, trying to work out how it went from me and Mom and Dad, mostly happy, to Hank beating me up as we drive down a deserted road. "Remember when I rode a bike for the first time? You holding onto my seat, running next to me, letting me go only when you were sure I'd make it on my own, then running alongside me anyway, just in case I fell?"

Hank takes a big swig from his bottle.

"Remember—" My voice hitches and I raise my ten fat sausages to swipe at my cheeks. "Remember when we went to Lagoon and had our picture taken? How happy we were? Remember when we went to the movies on Saturday afternoons and shared popcorn? Remember how you loved me once? Loved Mom?"

I think about the pictures of Mom and Hank holding me in their arms, loving their baby, imagining all the things I could be.

"Remember when you gave Mom that camera? How you spent a whole week's pay on it?" Even if Hank doesn't remember, I do. It's one of my best memories, seeing Mom so happy.

Hank's sitting in his barcalounger, Mom on his lap. She's got her arms around his neck, hugging him tight. "Thank you, honey. It's perfect."

Mom's new camera is still sitting in the box while she hugs Dad. Pretty soon she can't not play with it, though, and gets up and starts reading the manual. That's boring, so she fires it up, puts in the memory card because it's digital and she can take a billion pictures without spending a bunch of money on film.

"Get in front of the tree, Lilybeans!" Click. Snap.

Mom nudges Hank. "Join your kid, would ya?" Hank does and pretty soon he's lifting me up on his shoulders. Click. Snap.

Mom takes our picture out in the snow, at the kitchen table, more in front of the tree, me in a bubble bath with foam covering me from head to toe. We go for a walk and she takes pictures of icicles, the neighbor's barking dog, an old house that half burned down a few months before. Click. Snap. Click. Snap. Click. Snap.

Hank straightens up and shakes his head. "The only thing I remember is the two of you leaving me and not coming back."

"You were hurting us. We couldn't live with you anymore. You chose us once, but then you chose Grandpa Henry. You hurt Mom. You hit her."

Hank takes a long drink from his whiskey bottle, then another. He swerves, almost driving us off the road.

"Why did you let me be with Margie all this time? Why didn't you kill me earlier?"

Hank raises his fist, but it's shaking now. He doesn't hit me, just lets it hang there until he puts it around the neck of his whiskey bottle again. His mouth hangs open a little, his eyes half-lidded. Pretty soon he's swerving all over, the SUV hitching from one side of the road to another. If there were other cars, we'd be banging into them. "All you need to know, Beans, is that we'll be together again real soon." His voice is soft, his words slipping around each other, like the night he killed Mom. Hank's decided and he's crazy and there's nothing I can do now but get away from him.

I look out my window and try to get a sense of where we are. We're driving slowly down a long stretch of empty road, open fields on both sides now. The moon is bright, lighting everything up as much as it can. There're no houses, no streetlights, no other cars, and I can't see if whatever's growing out in the fields is tall enough to hide me. If I even make it that far. I don't dare turn around to see how long ago we left the forest.

I focus on Hank, letting my body fill with my

own kind of rage. This man, this crazy man who made his choices, killed my mother. He changed me so much I almost went quiet for good. Not my fault. Hank's fault. "You are a worthless piece of trash, just like Grandpa Henry said. It's probably good he smashed your finger with that hammer. At least you had an excuse for why your paintings sucked." These words twist my stomach into knots.

Hank wrenches the steering wheel hard and pulls over to the side of the road. He throws Grandpa Henry's SUV into park, leans over, screams in my face. "Don't you dare, little girl!"

I lean closer until we're almost touching noses. I take a big breath, fill my lungs with his whiskey breath and remind myself the dad I once knew is gone. "Your father was a moron. You're a moron." Hank's fury is big, bigger than I've ever seen it. "Mom and me, we were smart for leaving you. We were never the stupid ones. We weren't worthless or lazy or anything else you tried to make us believe. Maybe we were poor, but who cares? Poor isn't the worst thing." One more deep breath. "Hank."

It's my using his name again that makes his eyes widen, makes him lean down to pull the gun from under his seat. He raises it up, wants to smash me in the head again, make me unconscious until he can get where he's going. I'm ready. I twist my arms around and make my numb fingers click the seatbelt lock. The belt retracts fast and I bring my foot up, kicking him in the face as hard as I can. His whiskey bottle shoots to the floor and lands on its side. The whole cab fills up with the overwhelming stench. Hank looks surprised for a second and then automatic reflexes kick in. He leans over to get his whiskey before it all spills out. That's when I start kicking. Hard.

I'm watching myself kick Hank as hard as I

can—on the arm, in the stomach, my heel coming down on his thigh. Everything the hollow is filled with—the anger, the relief, the love, the acceptance, the missing Mom—they're kicking Hank's ass until he has no choice but to open his door and get away before I kick him right through his window. Who knew I had so much gumption?

"Son of a bitch!" Hank says when he stumbles out of the car and into the road. He'll be unsteady on his feet, but his fury will help keep him just sober enough. I figure I've got seconds. I scramble across the seat and fly out of Grandpa Henry's SUV like my tail is on fire.

I hear, "Shit!" before I'm running across the empty road and right to the edge of the big field that's growing I-don't-know-what. I hope for corn, but when the moon drifts out from behind some clouds, I see it's something shorter. Wheat or barley or whatever they grow in big empty spaces. The field doesn't come up to the road like I thought and there's a steep embankment covered in weeds and sharp-looking rocks I'm going to have to run down. Or roll down. Or face-plant down.

I hear a *click-snap* behind me. It's not like Mom's camera. It's not a *click-snap* that says I'm loved. It's a *click-snap* that says Hank's got his gun pointed at my back. "You stay right there, Beans. This isn't how it's gonna be."

I decide Hank's right. This isn't how it's going to be. I launch myself into the air, commence the running and the rolling and the face-planting.

I'm making such a ruckus sliding down this hill. The rocks spinning up around me sound like big hailstones on the tin roof of some random shed. Now I'm the Tasmanian Devil. I add a laugh to my rock hail. Right out loud, I laugh. It's not flat, not odd. It's normal—tinkling, even. Alive.

Thanks to the moon lighting things up now and then, I catch glimpses of the landscape around me—the rock embankment I'm sliding down, the massive fields with their crops of whatever, the black forest we passed out of awhile back. I don't see a single light. There are no houses out here, not even a farm.

My body is scratched, beaten, tired. The soul I thought was gone, the heart I thought had disappeared, they're with me. They're aching to stay alive, to see my spastic four-legged star, to see

Nick, Margie, Sam and Dr. Pratchett again. I'm filled right up the brim with wanting to live.

I land on my back at the bottom of the hill and look up at the sky. I make a promise to the stars and the moon that I'll live a whole new life if I get through this. I'll stay away from the quiet place. I'll let the people I love in. I'll find a way to fit and I won't let the emptiness come again. I'll face it all.

In my mind, Mom's words come and tell me what she meant, what she knew for sure.

It's important you listen to me now.

Pretend I'm with you.

Hear my voice.

You are the best person I've ever known.

I wish so much I could hold a mirror up and show you what I see.

You are brave.

She is my courage.

I stay frozen at the bottom of the hill, listening closely. The wind sneaks under my T-shirt and tries to make it billow out. It bends whatever's out in the field, rustles the far-off trees of the black forest.

I lay there, thinking of Nick, feeling his necklace under my shirt, against my beating heart. Once sand, uncountable. Now glass, shattered grains. Fragments held together. Strengthening.

Rocks dig into my back, my butt, my legs. So many bruises, so much pain. But I feel it, fully feel it. There's no numb or buzzing or hollow—just pure, unfiltered pain.

I wait and it's a little like that night all over again. I listen for Hank's drunk rage, but it's silence out here. There's no vacuum, though. I'm fully alive, every nerve ending singing, every heartbeat felt, every scrape and bruise alive with their own complaining.

"Lily, don't do this. We'll be with your mother

again. Don't you miss her?"

Oh god, how I miss her. The missing has been my whole life since that night. But she doesn't want me dead. Mom wants me alive and fighting.

I can't trust my ears with my heart pounding this loud. His soft whisper might be a scream or it might mean he's just above me. I know he's close when the rocks he's knocking down the embankment smack up against my legs. There's a loud clang, another shower of rocks and then he's hollering, "No!" and "Where is it?"

I don't wait to find out what he's mad about (besides me just kicking his ass). I grab a fist-sized rock nearby and scoot into the field, hoping for a good place to hide. It's wheat, I think. The only way I'm staying out of sight is to keep on my belly. I flatten myself down, close my fist tight around my rock and wiggle my way farther in.

"This isn't how it's going to be, Beans." I have no idea where he is until I see a flashlight beam a few feet to my right. He's come prepared.

I wiggle farther to my left, watching Hank's flashlight bob fast toward something in the opposite direction. He must've heard a sound. Birds in the field or something. I take a chance and sit up, praying the rock I'm holding is sharp enough. I don't look down at what I'm doing, can't take my eyes off Hank's sweeping flashlight beam.

With my numb, fat fingers, I use the rock to stab at the tape squeezing my wrists together, then nearly scream when I get my arm instead. I make myself look down then and use the moonlight to find a good spot. I do and make a hole big enough to tear the tape and pull my hands apart. I'm flexing my fingers when I see Hank's flashlight bobbing this way again.

I drop to my belly and start wiggling fast toward the forest. It's a long way to go on my belly, but I don't have a choice now. Hank's bullet for me is gigantic. I wriggle, feeling the scrapes and scratches from the hard ground through my thin T-shirt. I stop after a bit so I can listen to the night and try to figure out where Hank's gone. I flip on my back and lift my head above the wheat just enough.

"Olly olly oxen free!" he hollers as his flashlight beam gets bigger. He's figured out I'm not on the other side, that I'm not birds spooked by his crazy searching.

I send out hope the wheat field will hide me and get on my hands and knees to make better time. I hear Hank behind me. His flashlight beam switches direction, lands a few inches in front of me. "There you are," he says. "You stay right there, Beans."

I don't stay right there. I get to my feet and run, pump my legs like I've been a track star my whole life. Right through the wheat field I run, trampling stalks some farmer took a lot of time to plant. I'm stuck in this one motion—running—and everything else gets pushed out. It's my whole life, running through this wheat field.

I'm halfway across when light surrounds me—Hank's unsteady flashlight beam, bopping up and down in time to his own running. I know the brighter the beam gets, the closer he is. I steal a glance back just in time to see him trip, see him fall on his face in the dust and wheat.

"Son of a bitch!" he says.

I can't help myself—I laugh. I laugh because the big bad boogeyman who's been hunting me all over Seattle just face-planted. I run and I laugh. However this ends, I am free now.

"Beans! Don't you laugh at me!" His beam has found me again and is busy lighting my path right to the forest. When I feel something hit my back, I know Hank's lost his gun. He wouldn't bother with rocks if he still had bullets. "Get back here! You don't get to make the decisions!" Hank throwing rocks. It's what he does best.

His flashlight beam swings wildly as he starts running again. The moon lights the rest of my way to the jagged wall of trees, to a forest I hope will hide me better than this wheat did.

All the adrenaline I felt getting away from Hank starts to leak out when I make it into the forest. My body is slowing and my head is pounding. I feel where Hank hit me, feel the blood, sticky inside my tangled hair. My side is on fire. I'm not used to running so far so fast.

I collapse behind a massive tree with roots bigger than me and start pulling the still-tight tape from my wrists. Sensation is coming back to my fingers and they're less sausagey now.

I see Hank's flashlight beam before I hear him muttering and swearing to himself. I can't move. My lungs are fiery tracks inside my chest—cars racing up, down, crashing, burning. I think maybe I'm going to throw up. Puke down the front of me, sure enough. Better, though. I can breathe again. Hank thinks I'm still running, so he does too. His flashlight shows me he's up ahead now, searching deeper in the forest.

I look down at my fat fingers, but I can't see a thing. The dark is thick in this forest. I think about Grandpa Henry's car sitting back there on the side of the road, about trying for it, wishing I'd thought to drive off when I had half a chance. My body tries to throw up again thinking about going back—dry heaves that make my side wrench. Stabbing, throbbing pain in my head wants me to lie down where I am. Trying for the car is out of the question.

Hank's flashlight bobs off to my right—up-down, up-down, swing left, swing right, back to center, up-down, up-down. Dizziness comes. I close my eyes, let my stomach settle, let the pain in my side have its say for a minute or two.

Hank's coming back this way. When I get to my feet, I don't like how shaky everything feels, how weak my body is. I put a hand to my head and probe where he hit me with the gun. It's sticky, a little mushy and sends a zing of pain all the way to my toes. I stumble forward, moving toward where Hank's already done his searching, hoping he won't go over the same ground, wondering if he can track me with all that booze making his brain swim.

Hank's flashlight lands a few feet to my right. He's going over the same ground after all, getting closer. The beam shines up a cluster of trees and a bunch of brambly looking overgrowth. Lit up for just that second, I see a hollow spot in the middle of it all, a little den I hope doesn't hold a family of foxes or groundhogs. I lurch forward, drop to my knees, stick my hand in and feel around. Empty. The entry is small, but inside feels bigger. I know I can fit. I know like I knew Mom and I would get the vanity through my bedroom door. A lifetime ago. I suck in my stomach and commence to wiggling my way in.

The brambly mass is prickly, painful. It scratches and pulls at my bare arms. I think it must be made up of more thorns than foresty overgrowth. I hold one hand over where Hank smashed me in the head and shove through. The entry is smaller than it looked, but the space inside is big enough so I can stretch out on my side if I want to. I can't sit up, but it doesn't matter. I need to watch for Hank's flashlight beam anyway. I move to the very back and feel the trunk of a giant tree against my bare skin. It's cool, comforting. I'm Brer Rabbit in my briar patch. I hope.

Hank's flashlight beam plays around outside my brambly front door. If he drops to his knees, if he shines his flashlight in, I'm done. There's no backdoor in my makeshift cave. There's only one way out and he's blocking it. Blocking it with his bright flashlight, his insanity.

"Beans! Where are you?" He's using his cajoling voice, the "I'm being nice" tone just before he says something horrible. It's not his words I'm worried about now, though.

"Come on out, kiddo. I promise, I just want to talk some more. We don't have to see your mother just yet. Maybe we can make it work with Margie. The important thing is that we're together, Lilybeans."

If I didn't think it would hurt, I'd roll my eyes. I lay my head on the ground and press one hand to my mushy head, hoping he hasn't done any permanent damage up there.

I can't keep my eyes open. So sleepy. It's not like the buzzing. The buzzing's gone, for good now that I've answered. Just plain exhaustion. I try not to drift off, remind myself people who've had their heads smacked don't have any business sleeping.

Then staying awake isn't so hard when I hear Hank a few feet away. He's off to my right and, by the crunching of leaves, it sounds like he's settling in. I hear beeping and realize he's using a cell phone.

"You're going to want to listen to me, Marjorie," he says after a few seconds of silence. I can't hear Margie from here, but his voice carries in the stillness.

Hank laughs. "She's dead." He waits for a long time and I know Margie's screaming her head off. I can't hear her, but I know.

"Now, Marjorie, yelling and name-calling won't bring Lily back." His voice is sure, soft, sympathetic. His words don't slur at all. Even though I know he's insane, it's hard to understand how good he is at this, how convincing. If I didn't feel my heart beating, my stomach rising and falling with each painful breath, I might believe him too.

Leaves crunch underfoot as Hank starts moving again. My mind wants to take me back to that night, to remember the glass from Mom's pictures under his work boots. Not the time. I rub my eyes to help me focus.

Hank walks closer to my briar patch. I hear Margie now, tinny through the cell phone. "Lily! Please, sweetheart! Tell me you're okay! Lily! Lily!"

I put both hands over my mouth and let my tears out instead of my words. Margie's voice is so full of grief and terror that he's telling the truth. "Lily! Sweetheart, please! Oh god! Lily!" Hank walks away and I only hear Margie's sobbing now, the grief tearing at her heart, at her soul.

Hank laughs, then says, "See, Marjorie? Dead."

Margie screams, "No!" and it is the worst sound I've ever heard outside the *craaaack* of Mom's bullet.

I take my hands away from my mouth, my whole body shaking with the power of my silent sobs. Margie's terror, Mom's death, me changed—all of it because of him.

I hear a snap—Hank closing the phone, I think. I do the same with my mouth and make my body stop shaking. I listen through the pounding of my heart. I wait. The silence is strange again, abrupt.

Hank doesn't move for a long time. He's listening. I know he's listening. My phone starts playing its upbeat tune and pretty soon there's a rustling of leaves and his work boots coming down, smashing the phone mid-melody.

"I can wait," he says. By the softness in his voice, I know he means it.

The morning is dim inside my bramble cave. When I look toward the opening, though, I see massive trees and a leaf-littered forest floor right outside. The sunlight shines through the canopy, sending down beams Mom would've loved playing in. Dust motes, her favorite. "Dust faeries" she called them. Dancing and playing in a stream of sunlight.

I wiggle a few inches toward the opening and freeze. I've stiffened up in the night. This pain makes yesterday's feel like a skinned knee. I slept the whole night through and my body tells me that probably wasn't the best idea. My swimming head tells me I'm lucky I woke up at all.

I watch outside for a little while, stretching slowly to work out the kinks, trying to get a sense of what's happening, of whether Hank is still around. It's too quiet. I inchworm my way until I can poke my head out. The forest is lighter than I thought. It's thick trees, ancient pine needles and dead leaves as far as I can see. I think I hear a little rushing, maybe a stream or a river, but it might just be my ears. I look all around for Hank, see my cell phone, broken to bits now, scattered on the ground about ten feet away.

This is a huge forest, I see now. I could've run almost anywhere and hidden fine. A lot of the trees have those huge roots like I found last night. Like giants live in this forest, everything massive. I feel tiny in my bramble cave, safe, secure. I'm glad I fit.

There's no sign of Hank, but I move by millimeters anyway. The little bit of crunching under my hands is deafening in this forest of silence.

I take my time wriggling out and stay on my hands and knees just in case I have to wriggle back in. Nothing. No sound, no sign. My legs shake when I try to stand and my head throbs, reminding me that Hank came with his gun after all.

Everywhere my skin is bare is covered in long, beaded scratches. Blood has re-colored the new pink dragonfly T-shirt Margie bought me to brown and red. Bruises are just starting to show up, the darkest ones left by Hank's punches. I touch my hair, feel it standing on end, matted with dirt and dried blood.

I lurch toward the field we ran through last night, glad now I'm not too far into the forest. The wheat is my only point of reference. The forest is too dense, too disorienting, too big. I'll have to walk the tree line or go through the wheat field to get back to the road.

I stand in the thinning trees at the edge of safety and look at the open field. The wheat, golden and waving in the beautiful morning, reaches nearly to my waist and looks like a fluttery, welcoming road back to Margie, to Nick, to Binka, to Sam, to a life I want to be a part of now. I see the places where we trampled it with our running, with Hank's chasing. With my eyes I follow the feathery stalks all the way down our crushed path, up the embankment and back toward the road. I can't see Grandpa Henry's SUV because Hank parked it on the other side, but I have no doubt it's still there. Hank wouldn't leave without finishing what he started. Pretty soon a couple of people cross the street and look over the grooved and steep embankment. Men in light gray and dark gray uniforms. Cops.

I move slowly along the tree line, watching the men on the road to make sure Hank's not with them. He's got nothing to lose now and there's only one thing he wants. I make myself move by inches, deliberately, staying in the trees until I can't anymore.

I'm at the place where I'll have to climb up the embankment to get to the road or start heading through the field. The embankment on this side isn't as steep as the one last night, but it might as well be Mount Everest with the way my body aches and my legs shake. I wait for a minute, leaning against a big tree right there at the edge. I reach inside my T-shirt to hold Nick's necklace and look down at the shattered pieces of glass connected by little rivulets of metal, turning it this way and that. It's amazing to me—Nick bought me a necklace that says everything I am. Broken bits and strong bits forged together to make something whole.

"There she is," Hank says from behind me. I turn too quick and yelp when pain stabs at my head. He's walking through the forest, grinning, raising his hand. No rocks this time. Hank's found his gun. His eyes are all lit up, bright onyx that tells me he's happy he can finish his business now. "I had bigger plans, but this'll have to do," he says just before I see the gun's giant, round hole come up level with my head. "I hope this makes him happy enough to leave me alone. I hope this is good enough."

My body wants to stay frozen, to give in, to just lie down and let him finish. It's tired and in more pain than I thought a person could feel and still stay alive. But my mind tells me I have a chance. There are people here now. I'm not alone. I have to try. For Margie, Nick, Binka and Sam. For Mom, I have to try.

I push away from the tree and stumble-jog into the wheat field. I wave my hands over my head, screaming as loud as I can. I scream my pain, fear, hope, love, wholeness. I scream my life.

I hear Hank fire, feel a sting along my arm, keep my eyes on the wheat field, on the path back to Margie. The cops are all lined up along the side of the road, four of them now, getting bigger as I get closer. They have their guns out, pointing at Hank behind me. Puffs of gray float in slow motion, little ribbons of smoke from their guns.

I drop to my belly, gunshots echoing around me as I come to rest in dust and trampled-down wheat. The stalks feel like feathers against my cheeks, tickling the places that don't hurt, soothing the places that do.

"Hold still, Lilybeans."

"But it tickles, Mama."

"I know, baby, but we've got to get you dressed."

"Why do I have to be the bird? It tickles too much."

"You're the bird, sweet girl, because you know how to fly. Better than everyone, you know how to raise your arms in the air and make us believe you're a bird."

"Why, Mommy?"

"You know how you don't like to see the animals in cages at the zoo?"

"Yeah."

"You know how you believe in your heart they should be free?"

"Uh-huh."

"That's why, kiddo. You'll understand better when you're older, but, for now, believing that birds are meant to fly makes you the best girl to play one. Okay?"

"It still tickles."

"Yes, sweetie."

I roll over, put one arm over my eyes. All I can think is *please let it be over*.

Feet skid down the embankment where I made a shower of pebbles last night, one voice talking to someone not here, someone who will send an ambulance, two voices calling out for me. They're trampling the wheat stalks now, making their own path. I get my hands behind me, get into a sitting position so I can see better. I feel woozy, but the wheat is too tall and I need to see. I stand and look toward where Hank was the last time I saw him. I see a heap of unmoving flannel across the field, paint-splattered work boots stretched behind, the shiny metal of his gun glinting in the sun next to his limp hand.

I sit down hard and feel the pain in my head only a little before blue sky starts to slip away and gets replaced by darkness.

This place where I am now is dark, but not silent. I hear something metallic. Soft voices. Rustling. And Mom's words.

If you're reading this, it is for one of two reasons.

No matter how old you are, it's too soon.

Listen to me now.

Pretend I'm with you.

Hear my voice.

I'm trying to find the courage.

I'm not brave like you are.

You are the best person I've ever known.

I wish so much I could hold a mirror up and show you what I see.

With all my heart, I love you.

And new words.

Come back to us, Lily.

We miss you.

We love you.

Margie's voice whispering, saying words for more than just her. Smoky wisps of fog, silky tendrils that make my heart ache, make my mind wake.

The sun is bright in this hospital room. I sit up and look around. Margie's asleep in a chair next to my bed. Her face is white except for red spots high up on her cheeks. Mom's letter, back in its envelope, sits on her lap.

And Mom. She's sitting on the end of my bed, cross-legged and smiling in a beam of sunlight. Dust faeries dance through her while her hair floats like a halo around her head. I want to touch it, to feel the soft cotton balls on my fingertips again. I want to wrap my arms around her. Once more. Tell her I miss her. Tell her she was brave. Tell her it's okay we didn't have very long. The time we had was everything. I say these things in my mind, sobbing out loud as Mom fades, a last glimpse of the person I loved most in all the world.

Margie sits up, her eyes huge. "Lily!" she says when she catches her breath. "Are you okay?"

I nod, but the grief has taken my voice. I let it all out. Let it fill the room, the world. She waits with me while it all comes out, patient, knowing this is how it has to be. I think about Hank, about him not calling and me thinking he did, about the blood and Mom's body on the floor, about ketchup packets and Christmas wreaths and more photos than I can count and dog food factories and parks and meadows. I think about spreading Mom's ashes and going to the cemetery and Margie saying words to let go of her anger. I think about wheat fields and forests and Grandpa Henry's SUV, about insanity and choices and Margie and Hank's growing up time and deciding to let the hollow go, to feel again.

Most of all, I think about the pineapple, about what Mom said. I slice into my armor, get at the fruit. I examine what's in me. The hollow has stayed gone. I'm filled up, right up to the top of my head.

Dr. Pratchett was right. There's room for everything.

The grief finishes up its violent business and I lean back against my pillow, exhausted.

After a bit I realize there's a big bandage covering my arm where Hank's bullet came after all. "Aunt Margie, is Hank dead?"

She watches me for a long moment. "No, honey. The police officers shot him. He's in the critical care unit. Upstairs."

"Will he live?"

She takes a deep breath and squeezes my hand. "They don't think so, sweetheart."

"Okay."

"Are you all right? Should I get the doctor?"

"No, I'm okay." I look around the room, at a big bunch of Gerber daises on a table next to this bed. "From Nick?"

"He wanted to come," Margie says. "But his parents didn't think it was a good idea."

"I understand."

We're quiet for a minute, me looking at the blanket on my lap, Margie holding my hand.

"Aunt Margie, is—" I take a deep breath. "Is Sam okay?"

"He's fine. According to him, Binka's the new queen of his house. You'll be lucky to get her back."

My whole body breathes and my mouth stretches into a big smile when I think about how fat and spoiled Binka will be when Sam's done watching her. Margie's expression is surprised. She looks like she's seeing me for the first time. "You're more than okay, aren't you, Lily?"

I nod. "I'm more than okay. I'm good now. There's room for everything."

"What happened out there?"

"Hank went crazy. I mean, more than we thought, you know?"

She nods.

I look around this room again, see big trees outside the window, like we're sitting in the middle of the forest. This hospital room, a white and blue bramble cave. "Where are we?"

"Oregon" Margie says.

"Hank was taking me to Grandpa Henry's?"

She looks at her lap.

"It's okay, Aunt Margie. I'm okay now. Please tell me."

She glances past me, out the window. "Yes," she says. "Back to my parents' old house."

"Where it all started."

"Yes," Margie says. "Officer Archie had already been through there a couple times, but there was no sign of him."

"Because he was in Seattle with us, painting our pictures."

"Yes," Margie says.

"He wanted us to all be together again. Me, Mom, Grandpa Henry, Grandma Josephine. He was going to kill me there."

Margie closes her eyes for a minute, then opens them again. We don't say anything more about Hank's beliefs or his choices or his going crazy. We let silence fill the room, let the clang and clatter of the hallway remind us where we are. We think our separate thoughts, maybe Margie about the next box she wants to make.

Me, I'm thinking about Nick, holding his necklace in my palm, looking at all those tiny fragments, strong because they don't count on just themselves to stay together.

Hank starts to go to his own nothing place in the early morning. He's in a windowless hospital room, no pictures on the wall, handcuffed to the bed rail. Hank tethered to metal, just like he has been his whole life.

Margie and me, we're with him, together on one side of his bed. I'm holding Margie's hand tight.

Hank's face is slack, all the crazy gone, his eyes closed. Right there in his smooth skin, in his relaxed expression, I see the dad I loved, how Hank could have made different choices, different decisions. It's not just that he had a bad start. Margie did too. It's what he chose—the whiskey, the meanness, the decision to not fight what he knew was wrong. Hank believed Grandpa Henry. He lived down to his expectations.

In the smoothness of Hank's face, I see

something I didn't know before. When our last breath goes, we aren't rich or poor or mean or nice. We're just people who've lived for a little while, some of us in dog food houses with loving moms, some of us in mansions with cruel dads. Maybe when we die we're back to that starting place where the only thing that matters is what we leave behind.

Margie squeezes my hand. "They found something in his car I thought you might want to keep." She reaches into a bag she's got slung over her shoulder, brings out a camera and hands it to me.

I flip it over, touching where Mom touched, running my thumb over where she painted her name in fingernail polish. Rachel. I bring the camera up, look through the viewfinder, find my view. A little window to capture moments, to capture the how's and the what's and maybe even the why's. Mom with her knowing that explanations wouldn't come, sorries wouldn't be spoken. Mom with her knowing the little moments are all we have. Years of little moments captured with this camera. Years of everything that was, of everything she left behind. They'll stay with me more than Hank's meanness. I know because I will always remember.

Margie and me, we let our questions go with Hank's last breath. He doesn't wake. He doesn't explain. He doesn't say he's sorry. He just goes to his own quiet place.

I'm sitting cross-legged on my blue and white bed at home, Dr. Pratchett's workbook open in front of me. My fingers brush the silky paper and I remember how they drummed my open history book all those weeks ago, remember that story about the guy who stood up against a bunch of tanks because he didn't think what his country did was right. A brave man.

I trace the title of the chapter I'm on—*Checking in with Yourself*. Dr. Pratchett says I've come a long way, but I've got a long way to go and this workbook will help me get there. I think with the bees gone, Hank and the not-Hanks gone too, Dr. Pratchett's right. There's peace now, but it's not from the quiet place. It's from finding out why I needed it in the first place.

When my eyes start to droop from reading

about how to check in with myself, I get up off my bed and grab the box Margie made special for me. It's a big one and was supposed to be for my birthday next month. She decided I should have it early because she couldn't wait to give it to me. It's her prettiest one yet. The metal doesn't look like metal at all. It's a chocolate brown—my favorite—and it's smooth with these little green beads Margie says are made of sea glass running all the way around the bottom. Margie's used Chinese lettering again to etch a message into the lid. *Bravery* is what she says the beautiful characters mean. I run my fingers over the straight lines and the curly tails and think about the tank guy again.

When I open Margie's beautiful creation, there are treasures inside—Mom's camera, Nick's necklace when I'm not wearing it, Hank's picture of me and Margie in the meadow and some of Binka's kibble from when I forgot to put the lid back on.

Nick's necklace is on top of Hank's picture. I take it out now and hold it in my palm. This box Margie made me, Nick's necklace, Mom's camera, the new people in my life, these things tell me something I didn't know before.

I'm all wrapped up in love.

The light outside is turning orange. I hurry and slip Nick's necklace over my head, grab my phone and dial him up on my way to the patio.

"Hey," he says. "Thought you might miss it."

"I wouldn't miss it for anything," I say softly. "Here we go." The sun's orange glow descends over the tall buildings first, down their sides, right across the earth like someone's turned on a big lamp. Not an explosion of light, nothing so dramatic. A peaceful blanketing where everything's lit, glowing, silent.

ABOUT THE AUTHOR

Photo by Jamie Hudson Photography

Joann Swanson was born and raised in Ogden, Utah, where she attended old Catholic schools with spooky boiler rooms and even spookier nuns. These things have understandably influenced her dark novels.

She now lives in Boise, ID with her husband and three spoiled feline divas. She works full time as an instructional designer, teaches two classes for a university and writes every chance she gets.

Besides writing, teaching and designing, Joann is an avid reader of just about every genre (plenty of YA, a smidge of Sci-Fi, buckets of horror, a dash of literary, even some graphic novels).

Occasionally Joann and her husband try to remember that work isn't everything and do a big vacation—so far, Victoria and Vancouver BC, Vegas, the Oregon coast and Maui. Someday they hope to go to Sunnydale, CA. Why? Because Hellmouth.

Tin Lily is Joann's first novel.

Website: crankyowlbooks.com

65540923R00162

Made in the USA
San Bernardino, CA
04 January 2018